RETURN FIRE

Johns Hopkins: Poetry and Fiction
John T. Irwin, General Editor

RETURN FIRE

Stories by Glenn Blake

The Johns Hopkins University Press
Baltimore

This book has been brought to publication with the generous
assistance of the G. Harry Pouder Fund.

The Johns Hopkins University Press
2715 North Charles Street
Baltimore, Maryland 21218-4363
www.press.jhu.edu

The following stories have been previously published: "Shooting
Stars," *Night Train*, Fall 2002; "Return Fire," *The Hopkins Review*,
Summer 2008; "When the Gods Want to Punish You," *Boulevard*,
Summer 2009.

Library of Congress Cataloging-in-Publication Data

Blake, Glenn.
    Return fire / Glenn Blake.
       p.   cm. — (Johns Hopkins, poetry and fiction)
    ISBN-13: 978-0-8018-9431-2 (hardcover : alk. paper)
    ISBN-10: 0-8018-9431-X (hardcover : alk. paper)
    1. Southern States—Social life and customs—Fiction. I. Title.
    PS3552.L34825R48 2010
    813'.6—dc22   2009023831

A catalog record for this book is available from the British Library.

*Special discounts are available for bulk purchases of this book. For
more information, please contact Special Sales at 410-516-6936 or
specialsales@press.jhu.edu.*

Karen

In Memory of William J. McNeill

CONTENTS

RETURN FIRE

RETURN FIRE

He's sitting on the verandah, underneath the magnolias. The sun's going down. His backyard's in shadow. The sun's shining on the bayou and on the levee bluff beyond the bayou.

He's sitting out there, sipping his mescal. None of this hokey Hollywood horseshit. None of this knocking back shots, chugging the bottle, worrying the worm. This isn't pulque. This isn't tequila. He likes to keep the bottle in the freezer so that when he pours the maguey, it's viscous—not quite liquid, not quite solid. He likes the smoky taste. He likes to watch the mescal move. It doesn't just sit there like bourbon. It doesn't bubble like champagne. It doesn't foam like beer. It slowly, practically imperceptibly, roils in the glass. It's like watching a tannic pond, its bottom lined with leaves—days, weeks, months—turn itself over.

Angela loved the magnolias. She loved to sit out there. She loved to open the windows in the springtime and let the breeze from the bayou fill the house with that sweet Southern smell. She loved to pick a blossom and float it in a bowl and place the bowl between them during dinner. But they died so quickly, those magnolia blossoms, overnight, so in the mornings, before he shaved, before he fixed breakfast, he scooped them out and tossed them over the verandah.

He's thinking these things when he notices a hummingbird hovering over his drink. He's thinking, Ruby throat. He's thinking, Female. No blood-red bandana. The hummingbird alights on the lip of his glass. She's considering the contents of his container. She starts to tongue the nectar.

I wouldn't, he says, and she disappears.

He pours himself some more mescal. No ice. One quarter lime. He watches the worm writhe in the bottle.

He notices the hummingbird feeder hanging in the magnolia. He positioned it so that she could see it from the kitchen window. The feeder's empty. The feeder's been empty these many months. He's thinking, Four shots water, one shot sugar. He's thinking, Four shots sugar, one shot water. Something gets boiled. He could probably fill it.

He's thinking these things when he notices the ruby throat visiting the magnolia. She visits each of the feeder's ports, and then she darts back over and stops right in front of him. She's just hovering inches from his nose. The whirring's so loud, so close. This isn't mescaline, this isn't peyote, but he can see perfectly—in slow motion—the figure-eight patterns of her wings. She's just suspended there. She's just watching him. He can see her blink. Sorry, he says, and the hummingbird feeder, hanging in the magnolia, explodes.

He hears the laughter from across the bayou. He doesn't need to look. It's the Bagwells. On the other side of the water. In the next county. What are they now? Juniors? Seniors? Varsity football. Twins. He knows that. Over at James Bowie. Old man Buddy's boys.

He drove over once to talk to the old man. There used to be a ferry on Ferry Road. You'd drive your truck onto the floating barge, unhook the chain, and then pull yourself across. But Carla had taken care of the landing, and the ferry had never been found. So now you had to follow the bayou down through the slough to the interstate.

Sometimes an hour depending on the tides. You had to cross over the Old and the Lost, drive past rice field after rice field, down farm-to-market roads, until you reached the cattle guard. The gate was always locked, so you had to climb over and try to make the mile back to the big house, back in the live oaks, before the big dogs found you and took you down. But his old man and old man Buddy had never gotten along, so he said, Fuck it, before he made it through the slough, pulled off the road, and turned around. He wondered what this country was like before there were ferries, before there were bridges. Bayous and swamps. Rivers and sloughs. No way in. No way out. Who in his right mind would've settled here?

They started out in junior high, climbing the bluff with their .22, shooting at things in the bayou. Snakes and turtles. Working their way up the food chain. Birds and squirrels. He finds rabbits and armadillos when he mows along the shore.

He hears the rifle. He hears their laughter. He looks across the water, and there they are, standing up on the bluff, wearing their black letter jackets. The kicker's resting the rifle on his shoulder. The quarterback's sporting bleached-blond hair. He's seen their pictures in the newspaper.

They're just shooting, he says. They ain't aiming.

The quarterback's bent over with his hands on his knees. He's laughing so hard he can't stand up.

He hears someone screaming, someone screaming next door. Gladys? He's just sitting there, watching the Bagwells. They're giving each other high-fives. They're just standing there, right out in the open. The sun's going down behind him, and what's left's shining across the bayou, up the bluff, and into their eyes.

What's wrong with you, he says, shooting into the sun!

Those two sure terrorized Angela. She had a doe back then that came by in the evenings and grazed in the bottom close to the bayou.

And before long there was a fawn too feeding down there with her mama. Angela sprinkled some corn for them, and he stood a salt block on a stump, and in the evenings they sat out there on the verandah and watched the doe and her fawn graze their way to the water until the sun went down, and the dark came up, and all they could see of the two deer were the bright white spots on the back of the fawn.

He remembers the afternoon when he came home from work, and her car was in the driveway. He opened the front door and said, Knock, knock and walked into the den and placed his lunch box on the bar. He remembers the back door was open, and when he looked down their yard to the water, there she was, her back to him, kneeling by the bayou. He remembers shouting her name, running down the yard, kneeling there beside her, and when she turned to look at him, she was cradling the fawn and crying.

He's thinking these things as he lifts his glass, and as he lifts his glass, the bottle of mescal explodes.

He's just sitting out there, staring at what's left of the bottle. The neck gone. The top half missing. He hears someone screaming, and in between the screams, he hears the laughter.

He finishes his drink. He pushes his chair away from the table. He stands, opens the screen door, and walks inside. It's dark in there, so he can see the hole in the screen where the slug tore through. He looks across the room at the cabinet and sees the shattered china.

He walks downstairs into the bedroom and opens the closet. He pushes the hangers of work clothes to the right and finds the side-by-sides, the over-and-unders, the semiautomatics, the pumps. The .410. The 20 gauge. The 16 gauge. The 12. He pushes the hangers to the left and finds the leather cases. The lever actions. The bolt actions. The .243. The .270. The .30-30. The .30-06. The Weatherby .300 magnum. He reaches in and removes the case.

He climbs the stairs and notices the stack of newspapers. He grabs one, and while he's at it, he grabs a cushion from the love seat. He walks into the kitchen and opens the pantry. He feels around in there until he finds the package with the cheesecloth. He leaves the dark kitchen, opens the screen door, and walks onto the verandah.

He tosses the newspaper into the empty chair. He drops the cushion onto the table. He rests the rifle case upon the cushion. He drapes the cheesecloth over what's left of the bottle. He moves his chair so that it faces the far shore.

The shadows have blanketed the bayou, have climbed the bluff to their feet. They couldn't see him now if they tried. The kicker hands the rifle to his brother. He points at something across the water. He shields his eyes against the sun.

He positions the cushion on the table. He unzips the case and removes the Weatherby. He removes the caps from the scope. He rests the rifle upon the cushion. He sits down.

He hears something pass through the tops of the magnolias, the riflefire, the dry, leathery leaves pattering down around him. He hears the kicker whistling. He sees him waving across the water.

I see you, he says. Don't you worry. He slams a shell into the chamber. He turns his baseball cap around. He looks through the scope until he finds them. He selects the kicker. He drags the crosshairs from head to toe. Skull, sternum, navel, groin. He's thinking, .300 magnum. He's thinking, Two hundred yards. He's thinking, Kneecap.

The quarterback's reloading. They're looking down the bayou, their backs to him. They're digging in the pockets of their jackets. The kicker's hooting and hollering.

Turn around, he says. His finger finds the trigger.

They're wrestling for the rifle. The kicker snatches it away.

Fine, he says. He's thinking, Left leg. He's thinking, Right leg. He's thinking, Back of the knee. And before he fires, he says, What you boys know about shooting?

He watches the boy's leg kick the ball through the uprights, lift him high into the sky, up over his head, flip him perfectly, and then drop him down on his back.

No more field goals for you, he says. No more extra points.

He hears someone screaming, except this time it's coming from across the water. The quarterback falls to his knees. He grabs his brother's jacket and drags him down the other side of the levee.

He slams another shell into the chamber. He scans the bluff to the north. He scans the bluff to the south. He's looking for a blond head, a black torso, a rifle pointed in his direction.

He hears someone screaming. He hears someone shouting.

He rests the rifle upon the cushion. He grabs what's left of the bottle. He fishes around in the bottom for the largest shards of glass. He feels around in there with his fingers.

He drapes the cheesecloth over the jagged edge. He grabs the newspaper and removes the rubber band. He doubles the rubber band and then stretches it over the cheesecloth. He tugs at the corners of the cloth so that the fit's snug, the surface taut. He pours himself another drink.

The sun's gone down. The shadowline's made the Sabine by now. Louisiana maybe. Mississippi soon. Everything in the evening becomes the same black. The barn. The yard. The trees. If someone were standing down there by the water, he wouldn't be able to see them. The bayou's shining like liquid mercury, reflecting perfectly the same smooth silver of the sky.

The scope's almost useless now. He scans the still surface to the north and to the south for some disturbance, for some ripple, for someone wading across to flank him.

He's sitting out there on the verandah. The bottle's empty. The rifle's propped against the door. He hears the cicadas on every branch, in every tree, and if he listens carefully, he can hear the crickets beneath the cicadas. He hears someone sobbing through the darkness.

He's sitting out there, watching the fireflies drift across the water.

The night's thick with them. He tries to follow the fireflies between flashes. Here—one thousand one, one thousand two—there. He sees things sometimes. The barbecue. The birdbath. The barn. The bottom's filled with a bright green fog.

He notices a pair of headlights shining on the levee. He sees these lights before he hears the tires on the oyster shells. A vehicle. A visitor. Over next door. At Gladys's. He watches the headlights dance down the levee as the vehicle follows the bend in the driveway.

He hears the engine stop, a door open, the wailing now. He hears a man's voice, a consoling voice. He can't hear what it's saying, but he can hear the tone, and he can just imagine. Hush, now. Settle down, now. Everything's gonna be all right.

He watches a spotlight scour the levee, climb the steep embankment, and then stop. He sees something on the other side of the water, a magnificent buck, glaring across the bayou, standing up there at the top of the bluff.

Everything's dark again. The backyard. The barn. The bottom. The night has a way of healing itself. He hears the bullfrogs from down around the bayou. He hears the man's voice—questions now—rising at the end of every line. He hears a car door close, the engine start, the patrol car ease along the fence line.

He's listening for the tires on the cattle guard, the tires on the highway. He's listening for the tires on his oyster-shell driveway. No headlights this time. No bright spotlight. No flashing red lights. Someone's coming. Someone's passed the gate. Someone's coasting across the lawn.

He's thinking, I'm next. My turn. He's thinking of the rifle propped against the door. One shell in the chamber. He's thinking, When was the last time we had company?

He watches the patrol car pass through the carport. He watches the deputy park behind the house. He's thinking, He killed the motor. He's thinking, He coasted back here. He looks down from the verandah and sees a face in the window, an elbow resting on the frame.

He hears the cicadas, the crickets, the ticking of the engine cooling. He hears someone clear his throat and then, Bobby Dean?

Austin, he says.

Nice night, Austin says.

Quiet, he says.

Quiet *now*, Austin says.

He hears Gladys shouting in the distance, Come on in, babies! Come on in!

How you been? Austin says.

I been fine, he says.

I wonder, Austin says. I wonder.

He hears Gladys singing through the darkness, Nighty night. Sleep tight.

We're all worried, Austin says. We're all worried about you.

I don't doubt it, he says.

He sees the lights go out next door. The corral. The barn. The pen. The porch. He sees the bedroom light come on, shining every night from the back of the house, shining through the same pink drapes since he was a boy.

Somebody bagged one of the Bagwell boys, Austin says.

Imagine that, he says.

The special teams player, Austin says. The kicker. Shot him in the leg. The right leg. Blew it right out from underneath him.

It's a mean world, he says.

Right over there, Austin says. Across the bayou. On that bluff. You been out here long?

Tonight, he says. The afternoon. Most of the day.

You hear anything? Austin says.

Some shots, he says. Those boys. Some gunfire. No more so than any other day.

Shot one of Gladys's kids, Austin says. Killed one of Gladys's kids.

No shit? he says.

One of her goats, Austin says. Killed one of her goats.

That Gladys loves her goats, he says.

We're thinking, .22, Austin says. We're thinking, .22 Long Rifle. What do you think?

.22, he says.

You hear anything else? Austin says. Any heavy artillery? We're thinking, Someone with a big rifle. Someone with a big gun.

A big gun, he says.

You still got that .300 Mag? Austin says. You save that Weatherby?

That Weatherby saved me, he says.

That boy, Austin says. I wonder if he'll walk.

He won't come limping back out to that bluff, he says.

I wouldn't think, Austin says.

So much for scholarships, he says.

I guess it was time, Austin says.

It was *past* time, he says.

He sees the bedroom light go out next door. Goodnight, Gladys, he says. Everything's dark now. Even the fireflies have gone to bed. Lloyd and Maxine, he says. How are they?

Fine, Austin says. Just fine. They're always asking about you.

Appreciate it, he says.

Daddy comes by every now and then and picks up your papers, Austin says, but he says nobody ever answers the door.

I'm probably out back, he says.

That's what he figured, Austin says. He figured you were.

Maybe next time, he says.

Listen, Austin says, why don't you come out to the house? Why don't you come out Sunday?

Not just yet, he says.

Mama and Daddy, Austin says, they'd love to see you. They *need* to see you.

Not just yet, he says.

It might help, Austin says. It just might.

I don't doubt it, he says.

In the distance, across the bayou, he hears the call of the barred owl, Who cooks for you? Who cooks for you all? He hears Angela's tambour on the mantel chime the late hour. He hears the radio static from the patrol car.

Sjolander, he says. You think Sjolander'll drive over?

He'll drive out to the big house, Austin says. The Bagwell place. He'll drive up to the cattle guard, but old man Buddy won't let him in. He'll drive up to the big bridge, to the Old and the Lost, but then he'll turn around and head back home.

The last of his kind, he says.

The only sheriff in Texas, Austin says, that won't cross a river.

But old man Buddy, he says. Old man Buddy'll cross a river.

He's got his hands full, Austin says. Drove that boy into Beaumont.

Yettie Kersting, he says.

Yettie Kersting, Austin says.

I can take care of myself, he says.

Austin shines the spotlight down the oyster shell to the highway. I wouldn't let just anybody drive up this driveway, he says. Don't you got a gate?

A gate won't stop them, he says.

You know, Austin says. He shines the spotlight down the yard, across the bayou, up the bluff. I promised Sister I'd look out for you.

You have, he says.

I gave her my word, Austin says.

You can't save me, he says.

Austin kills the spotlight. Fuck it, he says. It's over. It's done. Ain't nobody crying about that boy.

Everything has a way of working itself out, he says.

Listen to me, Bobby Dean, Austin says. He starts the engine. You take care of yourself, he says. He shifts into gear. You keep your eyes open.

Tell your mama and daddy I said hey, he says.

I'll do that, Austin says and drives away.

He's sitting out there on the verandah. He's listening to the tires on the oyster-shell driveway. He's watching the taillights disappear in the distance.

The sounds of the night return. The cicadas. The crickets. The bullfrogs from down around the bayou.

He hears the patrol car cross the cattle guard. He hears the creak of the gate. He hears the clatter of the chain.

Listen to me, Austin, he says. In this life, we don't always get what we want. We don't always get what we need. In this life, we get what we deserve.

DEGÜELLO

"Six until midnight," he says as we pass.

"Drive on," I say.

"Drive on?" he says. "Into the Channel? Where are we going?"

"1836," I say. "Here," I say. "Take a right up here."

He turns off the highway onto 1836, the road lined with live oaks. The magnificent monument, the shellstone star, shine bright white. He stops the cab outside the main entrance.

"Eight until eight," he says.

"Drive on," I say.

"It's two in the morning!" he says. "It's *past* two in the morning!" He hasn't turned around. Even in the dark, I can see his eyes in the mirror. "What about the rangers?" he says. "The . . . patrols?"

"Midnight and dawn," I say. "Drive on."

"Where are we going!" he says.

"We're close," I say.

"To what!" he says. "Massacred Mexicans!"

"'There the bodies lay,'" I say, "'turning to skeletons which grazing cattle chewed for their salt.'"

"Do you hear me?" he says. He turns in his seat. "One mile!" he says. "My ass is taking you in for one mile!"

"Take a right," I say. "Take a right on the road to New Washington."

"New Washington?" he says. He takes a right. "I grew up around here. I grew up in this part of the country, and I ain't ever *heard* of New Washington! You sure you're in the right state?"

"It's a town," I say. "It *was* a town. Some two hundred years ago. I don't know. Maybe it slid off into the bay."

"I'll tell you where this road goes now," he says. "No town. No place. Nofuckingwhere."

I roll down the window and take a deep breath, and for the first time I smell the sloughs, the bayous, the rivers, the bays. "The Gulf of Mexico," I say.

I look off across the dark prairie to the marsh in the distance. "Mirabeau Buonaparte Lamar," I say. "This is almost the exact route of his cavalry as he cut off the Mexican retreat."

"Is that right?" he says. "Listen," he says, "why don't you let me take you back into Houston?" He turns around and looks at me. "Why don't you let me take you back into . . . *Shit!*" He slams on his brakes, and my head slams into the window frame.

"What!" I say, rubbing my head. "What is it!"

"The end of the line," he says, and then I see it. I see the road disappears under the water. The road disappears under the bay.

I open the door and step out of the cab. "Hit your brights," I say.

"What?" he says.

"Your bright lights," I say. "Your high beams."

The entire battleground is underwater. The complete battlefield submerged, from the Mexican breastworks, from Santa Anna's camp, all the way to the bay.

The road becomes a turnaround, an oyster-shell loop around a granite marker. He follows it with his cab, the back door open.

Some half a mile across, I can see where the road climbs out of the water, up toward the ridgeline, back toward the bayou.

"Hop in," he says, pulling up beside me. He has his window down. He has his elbow out.

"Is it high tide?" I say.

"Do I look like a sailor?" he says.

"I mean, I wonder how *deep* it is."

"No way!" he says. "No fucking way! It's company policy: 'Under no circumstances—under no circumstances at all—are you to ever even consider driving your taxicab *underwater*!'"

"How much?"

"What?" he says.

"How much do I owe you?"

"Hop in," he says. *"Let's get the fuck out of here."*

"How much?" I say, untying my shoes.

"I ain't leaving you out here!" he says. "No phone. No one for . . . ten miles. Fifteen miles. No one *living*! There's nothing out here!"

I take off my shoes. "You don't see it, do you?"

"See what?" he says.

I take off my socks.

"You're swimming across, are you?"

"Wading across," I say. "It can't be *that* deep."

"Come on and pay me then," he says. "Come on and pay me before you go and drown yourself."

I pay him the fare. "It's only death," I say.

He laughs. "That's right," he says. "That's *all* it is," he says. He shifts the cab into drive. "And it's waiting for your ass at the bottom of the bay."

I rest a foot on the granite marker. I roll up a pants leg. I can see the red taillights following the road back to the entrance, back to the highway, back to Houston. I roll up the other pants leg. The cab gone now.

I look across the water to the far shore. There are no lights. There are only long, low silhouettes of live oaks mirrored in the bay. A southeast breeze coming in from the Gulf. A gull? A tern?

"Where's your car!" I hear him before I see him. I'm walking down Battleground Road, my pants wet, my shoes in my hand, when he hits me with his spotlight and shouts, "Where's your car!"

"In Baltimore!" I shout back, shielding my eyes.

"You walked in from Baltimore, did you?" I can see him now, standing up in the tower, at the top of the ladder, in the door of the wheelhouse.

"I *flew* in," I say. "I *flew* into Hobby." I stop at the landing. The chain is up. Painted on each side of the tower is the word, "Lynch."

"That's quite a hike in itself," he says. "What is that? Twenty-five, thirty miles?"

"Twenty," I say. I can see him leaning on the banister, both hands resting on the railing, the life preserver on his left side, the spotlight on his right. "Permission to come aboard."

"Not just yet," he says. There is exactly one Laughing Gull on each of the posts of the landing. "Not just yet."

"I could step over this chain," I say.

"And I could blow your ass back!" he says, and the gulls, scores of them, laugh hysterically. "I could blow your ass all over this boat!"

"Do you threaten every passenger who walks up?"

"That's just it," he says. "I ain't ever *had* a passenger just *walk up*. You're my first. And look at you! Barefooted! You say you just flew into town—you ain't got no luggage! And what did you do in your britches! Son, we don't have any facilities on board." The gulls erupt in a chorus of guffaws.

"Will you take me across?"

"What time is it?" he says.

"A quarter till six," I say. "Five forty-three."

"Seventeen minutes," he says. "In seventeen minutes," he says. He turns off the spotlight, steps into the wheelhouse, and closes the door.

"What happened?" I say.

"What?" he says. He removes our moorings, and we embark. Each and every last gull takes flight to escort us. They take turns diving into the froth of our wake.

"The battleground!" I say.

"What about it?" he says.

"It's underwater!" I say.

"Sunk," he says. He is a small man, wiry, burned down one side of his body. One half of his face looks like it has melted. His right arm withered. His right eye white.

"It sunk," he says. "This whole part of the country's sunk." He looks at me with his good eye. "Subsidence, they call it. Subsided some ten feet this century. The refineries up the Channel are to blame. They keep pumping out the groundwater. We keep sinking."

He is wearing a captain's cap. "Are you the captain?" I say. "The pilot?" I look up to the dark windows of the wheelhouse. "I mean, is there someone up there steering this thing?"

"You'll get there," he says. He is smiling. "If I was you, I'd start worrying about what's waiting for me on the other side." He points out into the wake, and I see the dark dorsals in the white froth. Dolphins? Sharks? "I'd put my shoes on," he says, "and I'd tie my laces tight!" He takes off toward the bow, a slight limp in his gait, and I take off after him.

"Why?" I say.

He is standing at the bow, looking out over the water.

"What?"

"I don't think you know where you're going," he says. "I don't think you know what's waiting for you."

It is almost dawn, and I look to the light in the east and see what he sees—not a sunrise, not a sun coming up, but a fire—a big fire burning on the far shore.

"What do you want?" he says.

"To get to the other side," I say.

He laughs. "When the gods want to punish you," he says, "they answer your prayers. Now you understand me. I'm taking you across. I'm taking you to the other side." He takes off his cap and waves it in the air, and the scores of gulls cry. "But me and my gulls," he says, "we ain't waiting. We ain't waiting for you. We're going back. Do you understand?"

"I understand," I say.

"There's nothing out there," he says. "There's no one out there anymore."

"No one?" I say.

"No one in his right mind," he says. *"Degüello,"* he says. "It means revenge, I think. Sweet revenge—something like that—for what the Mexicans did at the Alamo. It used to be a real showplace. The country club section of town. All the oil executives lived out there. Big houses. Big homes."

"I know," I say.

"But not anymore," he says. "Most of those houses are out in the water now. Most of those homes are out in the bay."

"What happened to the people?" I say. "What happened to the families?"

"Most of the old families died off," he says. "Most of them moved away."

"Are they all gone?"

"They ain't *all* gone," he says. "I think there's some holdouts, but

I shit you not, their asses are out in the water! Their asses are out in the bay! They park their cars on the levee road and take boats to their houses!"

"The city's shut the place down," he says, "barricaded the entrances, cut off the utilities, so there might be someone living in those homes, but like I said, no one in his right mind."

It is dawn when the ferry reaches the other side. Each and every last Laughing Gull lands just long enough for us to ease into the landing, for him to lower the chain, for me to step onto the shore before the ferry drifts back into the Channel, and they all take flight again.

"Last chance," he says, the ferry drifting farther. He reaches out with his good arm.

"Thanks for the ride!" I say.

He shakes his head, lifts the chain, and shouts across the water, "You won't like what you find!" He shouts, "Do you know what's waiting for you! Do you know what's over there!"

And I say, not loud enough for him to hear me, I say, "Home."

THANKSGIVING

Zebras. Tigers. Neon Tetras.
Angels. Devils. Runny Noses.
Snakeheads. Swordtails. Silver Dollars.

The tanks gurgling. I like the sound it makes. I like the blue rocks. I like the white castle where the little fish can go and hide.

I close my curtain. I turn my light off. I lie on my bed and watch the tank glow all day long. And at night, when everythings got quiet, when everybodys gone to bed, I lie there and watch the fish swim and listen to the bubbles till I fall asleep.

The door opens. Shithead, he says. Wake up.

Im awake, I say.

He turns the light on. Get your ass up, he says.

I climb out of bed. Its up, I say.

You sleeping in your clothes, he says.

I like to be ready, I say.

Lets go, he says. Its almost noon. He grabs me by my ear and leads me outside.

Almost noon, I say.

Its a bright day. The wreckers parked on the road. The doors open.

Wheres Squirt, I say.

Sleep, he says.

Wheres Mama, I say.

He shakes me by my ear. Dont you worry bout your Mama, he says. You hear me.

I hear you, I say.

He picks me up so Im up on my toes. Dont you go bothering her, he says. Dont you go winding her up.

I wont, I say.

He lets go. He reaches in his pocket and pulls some keys out. Go get your Gramma, he says.

Yesir, I say.

Take the duck truck, he says. Stay on the shoulder.

Yesir, I say.

Go get your Gramma and bring her back here, he says. Its Thanksgiving.

Thanksgiving, I say.

Go get your Gramma, he says. Take the duck truck. Stay on the shoulder. You think you can handle that.

I can handle that, I say.

Im going to the shop, he says. The turkeys in the stove. Ill be back afterwhile.

Afterwhile, I say.

He climbs in the wrecker. He closes the door and rolls the window down. He looks out at me. Dont hit nobody, he says. Dont let nobody hit you. You understand.

I understand, I say.

He starts the wrecker. I mean it, he says. You get in a wreck, you better be dead before I find you. You hear me.

No wrecks, I say.

Thanksgiving

If you dont die on the highway, he says, you can change the oil in the duck truck tonight. Can you do that.

I can do that, I say.

He shifts the wrecker into gear. He points his finger at me. Dont get yourself killed, he says and drives away.

I stand out there and look cross the road. Mr Rockwells got some turkey decoys. I can see them lined up on his porch. Squirt waits till the coast is clear. He waits till Mr Rockwell goes to work, and then he crawls underneath our house and shoots at them. He shoots at them till they fall over. Most of them look pretty close to dead. One aint got a head. One aint got no feet. Hes just sitting there on his bottom. Ones rolled off the porch and all the way down the driveway.

Daddys got a garage. He fixes things. Cars. Trucks. He fixes everything thats broke. He use to work at the house, but then Squirt came along, and EVERYTHING WENT TO HELL.

Squirt use to live with me till Mama got scared that Id kill him. Squirtll do anything you say. Jump off the roof. Jump out a tree. Eat everything. Bugs. Bad berries. Bullets. Pennies. Nickels. Dimes. Guppies. Glass. Hell stick marbles up his nose. Mamad hold him. Mamad run round the house and scream, YOURE GONNA KILL HIM. YOURE GONNA KILL HIM.

No I wouldnt. I wouldnt never. Squirts better than having a dog. Squirts like having a monkey.

So Squirt moved into the garage, and Daddy moved into town. Mama fixed it up nice. Painted it all blue. Cleared out a spot. Put a bed in there. Mama told me to tell Squirt not to touch Daddys guns. Not to turn his machines on. Not to play with his tools. So I told him,

Just in case you got any, dont go blowing your brains out.

Dont go cutting your fingers off.

Dont go drilling holes in your head.

Dont go sawing your body into.

I have to watch him every second, or hell do just that. So Squirt got the garage and the dogs and the guns, and I got my old room back.

I have a secret door. No one else knows bout it in the world. Its like a secret passageway. Its like a secret tunnel outside a dungeon. Its a hole underneath my bed. When everything gets bad in the house, when everyone gets mad, I can climb out of my covers, I can crawl underneath my bed and sneak out.

I walked out to the garage and got a hacksaw blade. I got a tape too and measured myself. I measured myself so that I could get out. I measured the dogs so that they could get in. I waited till Mama took her nap, and then I moved my bed and started sawing.

Mama takes a nap every day thats not a school day. Thats when everythings quiet. Thats when everythings calm. Some days shell sleep for hours, and on those days Ill sneak in there and saw. Its like Im a prisoner. Its like Im escaping.

Mamas a good mama as long as shes asleeping. When shes awake, THERES HELL TO PAY. I have to be careful moving the bed. I have to be quiet sawing the boards. If you wake her up, shell start screaming. Shell start throwing things. Shell start chasing you round, and if she catches you . . .

you wouldnt think it to look at her, but she can hit harder than Daddy. Shes a girl, and girls dont aim. Girlsll hit you where ever they can.

Mama aint got no teeth. Not one in her whole head. I looked in there while she was snoring. I got my flashlight that I take out to the blinds and shined it all over the place in there. Nope. One time she was cooking at the stove in the kitchen, and I asked her, Mama, why aint you got no teeth, and she whacked me on the head with a wooden spoon and asked me if Id like to have MY teeth knocked out.

Mamas got false teeth. Mamas got false teeth that she can stick in there and look like a normal person. She can just open her mouth and stick them in there. Theyre bright white. Theyre straight. There aint one cavity. There aint one filling. I asked her if they was human teeth, and she whacked me again.

She takes them out when shes asleeping. She can just reach in there and yank them out. Does it hurt, I say. When she takes them out, she looks like Gramma. When she takes them out, she sounds like a retard. I know not to laugh. But not Squirt. When Mamas awake, when shes storming round the house with no teeth in her head, somethings bout to happen. I know not to look at her. I know not to talk to her. But not Squirt. The second he sees her, the second he hears her talk, he falls on the ground and starts rolling all over the place, and then the dogs start barking, and then its time to run.

I tell Squirt you gotta keep your eyes open. You gotta keep your ears open. When Mamas mean, when shes awake, you better run. You better hide. When shes in the house, you better not be. You can be tending to your own rat killing, but youre bout to get beat.

I tell Squirt you gotta keep your mouth shut. Squirt dont talk. He can talk. He just dont. I tell him not to. Dont talk, I say. Dont say a word. You can talk to the dogs, and you can talk to me. You talk round here, and youre bout to get beat. It always happens. They shout at you. They scream at you. They ask you questions. And no matter what you say, youre bout to get beat. So Squirt dont talk. Daddyll pick him up by the ear. Daddyll shout in there, Is anybody home. Daddyll drop Squirt down on the ground and say, Just what we need. Nother retard.

It makes Mama mad. Shell pick Squirt up and start shaking him. Talk gotdammit, she says. When Mamas not hugging or kissing on Squirt, shes beating on him. I know you can talk, she says. Ive heard you with the dogs. Shell start shaking him hard, and Ill run up and hug her leg and say, STOP MAMA PLEASE. YOURE GONNA BREAK HIM.

This is why I hide Mamas teeth. This is whatll stop her. When shes beating on Squirt, when shes beating on me, I go for them teeth. Top and bottom. I get them teeth and hide them. In the attic. Under the house. In the dog food. In cans of paint. Buried in the ground. Sometimes when things get bloody, Ill forget where I hid them. Sometimes when were playing outside, up in the tree house, down in the ditch, well run cross a pair, and Squirtll scream, and Ill whack him on the head and say, Thats just Mamas teeth.

Mamas a school teacher. She teaches school. School teachers need teeth. School teachers cant teach school without no teeth. Mama cant teach school. When Mama cant teach school, SHE gets a beating.

I gotta keep my eyes open. I gotta keep my ears open. If I dont, shell catch me. Shell grab me by my throat and say, Where are my gotdam teeth.

And Ill say, Dont know.

And shell slap me down.

And Ill get up.

And shell say, Where are they.

And Ill say, Dont know.

And shell slap me down and go after Squirt.

And Ill get up and say, You beat him, and youll never see them teeth again.

Nobody beats Squirt but me.

I walk through the garage before I go. Squirts asleeping with the dogs. You boys look after him, I say. I walk through the house. The dining room. The kitchen. There on the bar is the church key and the four cans of oil for tonight. Mamas asleeping on the ground in the bath room. I open my door to check on my fishes. The rooms dark, but I can see the Chester drawers. I can see the blue tank glow. Jack Dempsey, I say, keep a lookout. And then I go.

I hate starting the duck truck alone. I gotta choke it. I gotta stomp one foot on the clutch pedal. I gotta stomp the other on the starter, and all this time Im rolling backwards down the driveway cross the road. Sometimes Ill roll over into Mr Rockwells yard. Sometimes Ill roll out into the road and almost hit someone. Sometimes someone almost hits me.

I gotta push the seat back. I gotta stand up when Im driving so that I can see over the dashboard. I stay on the shoulder. I stay in first gear. In the duck truck, the gearshifts on the column, and second gear is sitting right up there next to reverse. Daddy says all it takes is one time shifting from first into reverse, and youll never do it again. The scariest part is the signaling. I gotta let go of the wheel and stick my whole arm out the window.

I drive over the Trinity and through the Thicket to Grammas house. I drive through Ames where the Niggras live, where white people aint allowed to stay. I drive through the deep woods till there aint no trees just fields as far as you can see. Sometimes theyre filled with water, and you can see the blue sky. Sometimes theyre so bright green they hurt your eyes. The dirt levees snaking way off to the ends of the world.

I can see the men out there, black and white, working in the water. Everybodys got his own field. I honk my horn and wave at them. Mr Leo and his men. Mr Lloyd and his. Mr Bob and Mr Joe. Mr Bill takes his hat off and waves back. They all know this truck.

I drive through Raywood with its white castle. Its towers reach the sky. One day, I ask Daddy, Wheres the drawbridge.

Shut up, he says.

I mean it, I say. Where is it.

What, he says.

You know, I say. The drawbridge. The front door. Every castle has one.

You retard, he says. That aint a castle. Thats a dryer. Thats where they store the rice. Thats where they store the grain.

In case they get attacked, I say.

Shut up, he says.

When I get to Devers, I turn by the station with the big green Dino on top. One day, I point and tell Daddy, Thats a brontosaurus.

You retard, he says. Thats a dinosaur.

Mamas a school teacher. She teaches first grade. It use to be quiet. It use to be calm. Daddyd get up and go to the garage, and Mamad get up and go to school, and itd just be me and Squirt and the dogs playing all day. But then I grew up and had to go to school. The principle said it wouldnt be fair for me to be in Mamas room, so they stuck me in The Special Class.

The Special Class was great. Everything was Special. We had a Special lunchroom. Plastic forks and plastic spoons. We had a Special playground. A merry-go-round. A jungle gym. All rubber. Everything was short. Everything was close to the ground. Thats so we couldnt fall so far. Thats so we couldnt hurt ourselves.

We were always walking round the school. Lets go for a stroll, Miss Bingham says, and off wed go. All of us tied together with these ropes so that we wouldnt wander off. Wed walk by Mamas room, and Id knock on the window and wave at my friends that were having to sit in there and learn to read. We were always walking all over the place. Every now and then, theyd load us on a bus and drive us into Houston. Every now and then, theyd drive us to the circus. Every now and then, theyd drive us to the zoo.

The greatest thing was this. No matter what, you couldnt get in trouble. You could walk round all day with a trash can on your head. You could stand on the slide and scream. You could eat your crayolas. You could eat your paste. You could run round on your hands and knees barking like a dog. You couldnt get in trouble. Why. We were Special.

This week, we put our hand down on a piece of paper, and then we trace it, and then we color what we trace. We color the thumb red.

Thats the head, Miss Bingham says. We can give it a eyeball if we want to. We color the fingers with different crayolas. The fingers are the feathers, Miss Bingham says. We color the rest of the hand black, and what we got is a turkey.

I drive through Devers to Grammas house. She lives in the woods at the end of the road. I drive into her yard and shift into neutral. I honk the horn. The front doors open. GRAMMA, I shout out the window.

I climb out and run up to the porch. Gramma, I say.

I open the screen and walk inside. Gramma.

I walk through the living room. The dining room. The kitchen. The stoves on.

The back doors open, so I walk outside. GRAMMA, I shout into the woods, and then I see it, not my door open, but hers, and Gramma sitting in the truck.

I laugh and run out to her. I climb behind the wheel and say, Hey Gramma.

And she says, Woody.

Thats right, I say. I shift into first and gun it so hard it slams both our doors. I drive through the trees and back onto the road. Grammas staring straight through the windshield. Woody, she says.

Mam, I say.

I stay in first gear. I stay on the shoulder. I drive the twelve miles back home. And as we pass each field, I honk, and Gramma says, Bill, Joe, Bob, Lloyd, Leo, just like she knows them by heart.

I turn off the highway, down the road, and when I pull up front, I see Mama lying facedown in the yard in her underwear.

Woody, Gramma says.

Mam, I say, but I dont stop. We got plenty of gas, so I keep on driving, on into town and out the other side to the river bottom where we use to go to church.

Theres cars and trucks parked underneath the trees. I stop over by the graveyard and shift into neutral. I run round and open Grammas door, and she says, Sunday.

Nome, I say. Its Thanksgiving.

I walk her round back where the picnic tables go all the way to the river. I can see the red and white tablecloths. I can see the sleepy moss blowing in the breeze. I can see all my friends in their Sunday school clothes. Come and play, Woody, they say.

Not today, I say.

Mr Preacher walks up and says, Why, Sherwood, this is a surprise.

Yesir, I say, I expect.

Mrs Preacher walks up and says, Wheres your mother.

Resting, I say. This is my Gramma.

Mr Preacher says, Its a pleasure, mam.

And I say, Can she have some turkey with you.

Why, of course, Mrs Preacher says. She takes Grammas arm and says, Come with me, mam.

And Mr Preacher says, I hope youll join us, Woody.

And I say, Maybe next year. And I start running for the truck. Take good care of my Gramma, I shout back at him.

We will, he says. She can have as much turkey as she wants.

I climb in the truck and shift into gear. You gotta cut it up for her, I say. She aint got no teeth.

I turn the engine off. I shift into neutral and coast up the road. Shes still lying there in her underwear. I open the door, but I dont shut it. I tiptoe up behind her in case its a trap.

Mama, I say. I kick her foot. I walk round and round her. I stay way clear of her at first. She could jump me like a gator.

Hey Mama, I say. I poke her head with my boot. You alive.

Hey, I say. I reach in my pockets. I found these teeth in the back of the commode, I say. I put them together, top and bottom, and hold them in my hand. I squat down so that she can see them.

A car comes down the road and stops behind me. Sherwood, it says. Sherwood.

I stand up and turn round. Its Miss Bingham. Shes dressed up. Hi Miss Bingham, I say.

Is that your mother, Miss Bingham says.

I look at Mama. I think so, I say.

Is she all right, Miss Bingham says. Is she ok.

Shes just fine, I say. I bring my finger to my lips. I whisper, Shes just asleeping.

For gods sake, Miss Bingham says, put something on her. And then she drives away.

Shes right, of course, so I walk to the duck truck and climb in the bed. I find the camo tarp and throw it over Mama. I got her head covered with her feet poking out, and then I got her feet covered with her head poking out, and then I got her whole body covered when I see the front door open and the smoke pouring out.

Shit, I say and run inside. I cant see a thing. The houses filled with smoke. I fall over the coffee table. I get up and find the back door. I throw it open, and the dogs run in. Hey, I say. HEY.

Im swatting at the smoke, trying to find the fire. I run into my bedroom to check on my fishes. Everythings fine. The rooms dark. The blue lights on. No smoke in here yet. Water dont burn. I stick a towel under the door, and then I climb under the bed, and then I sneak through the hole, and then I crawl under the house.

I run into the garage. Squirts still asleeping, so I kick him and say, The houses on fire. The dogsre hopping up and down on the bed. Wake him up, I say.

I drag the box fan into the kitchen and turn it on. Im coughing. My eyesre burning. The fans blowing the smoke round. The dogsre jumping up and down. Wheres the fire, I say.

And then it hits me. The stove. I run over and open the door, and the black pours out. The dogsre barking now. Theyre going crazy like they want to climb in there. SHOO, I say. GO WAY.

I find the stove glove. I hold my breath. I close my eyes and reach inside. I feel the turkey, but its stuck to the pan, and the pans stuck to the stove. I yank and yank and rip it loose. The turkey looks like a burnt football. Im holding the leg till the leg falls off, and whats left of the bird falls on the floor, and the dogs jump on it like its a duck. Theyre barking at it. Theyre biting at it. Theyre snapping and snarling like they cant decide if they love it or hate it. They take turns dragging it outside. THATS GONNA BE HOT, I say. The turkey leg tastes just bout right.

I lift the garage doors, and the sun floods the room with light. The breeze from the rivers blows the smoke away. The dogsre out back with the turkey.

Shithead, I say. Wake up.

Squirt dont move.

You alive, I say. I kick him with my boot.

Squirts the best. He can play dead better than anybody. Even I cant tell. Its like he can stop breathing. When things get bad, when things get bloody, Squirt plays dead.

If youre dead, I say, you better tell me. I aint mouthtomouthing you. You can just die before I do that. You can just die and rot in here. You can just die and rot in here, and the dogsll eat you. You dont think Mama and Daddyll care. They wont care. I wont even care. Maybe the dogsll care, but itll be after they done ate you. Crying round, howling round, sad that youre dead, carrying you round in their stomachs to remind them.

Squirt aint breathing. His heart aint beating.

I aint shitting you, I say. Dont make me tickle you.

Squirt opens his eyes. He sits up. Morning, he says.

Its afternoon, I say. Get your ass up.

Hes rubbing his eyes. Wheres the dogs, he says.

Thingsre bout to get bloody, I say. We gotta get out of here.

Squirts out of the bed in one jump. Hes standing there in his pajamas with the trap door in the bottom. Lets go, he says.

Get in the truck, I say. Ill be there directly.

And hes gone.

I grab my flashlight that I take out to the blinds. I walk through the house one last time. Theres still black smoke pouring out the stove. I move the fan and point it inside.

I walk out back and climb under the house. I can hear the dogs before I see them. Theyre over there somewhere, snapping and snarling. One of them drags the turkey over to ask me if I want some.

No thank you, I say. I poke my head up into my bedroom. I peek my head out from under my bed. The towel worked. Theres no smoke. Jack Dempsey, I whisper, youre on your own.

Squirts in the duck truck. Hes got my door open. Lets go, he says. He stomps on the starter, and I stomp on the gas.

Squirt points at the tarp. Theres a foot poking out. Whos that, he says.

Thats just Mama, I say.

What happened, he says.

Thanksgiving, I say.

We drive through town. Get down, I say, and Squirt hides in the floorboard. The squares empty. The courthouses closed. Everybodys home and happy. We drive on out to Rivers Road.

You can get up now, I say, and Squirt climbs up in the seat.

Wheres my gun, Squirt says.

You mean you left it, I say.

We drive down Rivers Road to the Old and the Lost. Theres a place where these rivers come together and turn into the bay. Theres a place where Rivers Road ends, and you can stand there and look out as far as you can see. Every night Old River pours out the Thicket and pours into Lost River right bout here, and every night right bout here these rivers come together and pour one another into the bay.

I stop where the road runs underneath the water. I grab my flashlight. Squirt jumps out, and we meet at the end of the road.

Wheres my boots, Squirt says.

Hop on, I say. I squat down, and he hops on, and we wade out into the Old and the Lost.

What bout the gators, Squirt says.

Im walking slow and keeping my eyes on the water all round us. There aint no gators, I say.

But you said, Squirt says, you said theres always gators.

Not today, I say. Not on a holiday.

Im ankledeep, and then Im kneedeep, and then Im waistdeep when I see it. Squirts blinds way out there in the water. Its so hid sometimes I cant find it in the cattails. I see it now because of the buzzards. Theres four of them sitting on the corners.

Wheres my gun, Squirt says.

They dont fly for the longest time. Ive never been this close before. Theyre way too big to be birds. Theyre baldheaded. Theyre just sitting there watching us. I stop walking. I hold Squirt tight in case theyre thinking bout snatching him up and flying away.

GET ON, Squirt shouts in my ear, and they take off. They fly right over us. We can feel the wind in their wings. THATS RIGHT, Squirt shouts. GET ON AWAY FROM HERE.

Hey gotdamit, I say and swat at his bottom.

What, he says.

We climb into his blind, and we see why. Its filled with flies. Theres two stringers of dead ducks hanging from the posts. A noose round their necks.

Thats why, I say. I drop him down on the bench.

Thats where they went, Squirt says.

I untie the ropes. You cant tell what kind of ducks they were. You cant even tell that they were ducks. Somethings been eating on them. I hold them up in front of Squirts face.

Squirt holds his nose.

Its a sin, I say, not to clean your kill. I throw them off into the cattails, and something comes up out of the deep water with big teeth and snatches them.

Im sorry, Squirt says. I know better.

The fliesre gone.

Squirts sitting on the bench with his feet in the water. Stand up, I say. Dont do that.

Squirt stands up on the bench. Hes smiling. Is this a game, he says.

Yes, I say. Its a game. Its a mean game.

He stops smiling. Then I dont want to play, he says.

I know, I say. You dont have to.

Woody, he says.

Here, I say. I give him my flashlight.

But thats yours, he says.

Its yours now, I say.

He turns it on and shines it in my face.

Stop it, I say. Listen to me. I gotta get going.

No, he says.

I gotta, I say. Youll be safe out here. Dont leave this blind. Dont burn that till the sun goes down.

No, he says.

When everything gets quiet, I say, when everything gets calm, Ill come for you.

Its gonna get dark, he says.

I look all round me in the cattails. Keep your feet up out of the water, I say, and then I wade on back to shore.

Im waistdeep, and then Im kneedeep, and then Im ankledeep when I hear him shouting, DONT GO BACK. DONT GO BACK THERE.

I look back one last time, and all I can see of him is a little head poking up out of the duck blind, and I shout out, YOU BEST WORRY BOUT YOUR OWN SELF.

I climb in the truck and stomp on the starter. I shift into gear and look through the windshield. I cant see Squirt anymore. I cant even see the blind hid out there in the cattails. All I can see is the buzzards flying in circles up above the bay.

When I pull up to the house, Mr Rockwells standing in his yard. Hes collecting his decoys. Hes holding one like hes holding a baby. Hes frowning at me.

I climb out of the truck and say, I didnt do it. Which is the truth.

Everything looks pretty much like I left it. The front doors still open. The houses still smoking. Mamas still asleeping underneath the tarp.

When I walk inside, the dogs attack. They start jumping up and down. They start running round and round. I show them my hands. Turkey, turkey, I say. Gone, gone.

I walk down the hall and open my door. I reach down and pick up the towel. The rooms dark. The blue lights on. All the little fishes are hiding in the castle. Jack Dempseys swimming back and forth keeping guard.

Jack Dempsey, I say. I put my hand on the glass, and he swims over like hes trying to kiss it. Im very proud of you. You did a fine job.

And then I walk into the living room and stand at the bar. Theres the four cans of oil for tonight, theres Daddys church key, theres Mamas bottles, and theres the phone.

When he answers the phone, I say, Daddy.
And he says, Who is this.
And I say, Its me.
I know who it is, he says. This important.
Sir, I say.

Moron, he says, thisd better be important.

Yesir, I say.

Moron, he says.

Yesir, I say.

Is this important, he says.

You better come home, I say.

I dont think thats what you want, he says. I dont think you want me to come home.

I dont know what to say.

Do you want me to come home, he says.

Not really, I say.

And then he hangs up.

When he answers the phone, he says, The house on fire.

HOW DOES HE KNOW.

SHERWOOD, he says, the gotdam house on fire.

Sort of, I say.

Sort of, he says.

Sort of, I say.

Where is it, he says.

What, I say.

THE GOTDAM FIRE, he says.

The stove, I say.

Gotdam turkey, he says. Gotdam Thanksgiving.

I know, I say.

Squirt, he says. Get him out.

Hes out, I say. Hes safe.

The dogs, he says.

Out, I say.

Your Mama, he says.

Shes asleeping, I say.

Let her sleep, he says. Woody.

Sir, I say.

Dont catch yourself on fire, he says.

Yesir, I say.

Dont burn yourself to death, he says.

I wont, I say.

And then he hangs up.

Im standing outside when Daddy gets home. He drives the wrecker into the yard.

WHOA, I shout. Im standing in front of the tarp. WHOA.

He honks the horn. GET OUT THE WAY, he shouts. He jumps out of the wrecker and tramples over Mama. He walks right on top of her. He storms into the house, and I storm in after him.

The houses still filled with smoke, but he knows where to go. He stops at the stove, reaches in and grabs the pan, and throws it through the kitchen window. The glass breaks, and the dogs bark. They snap and snarl at the pan and then drag it underneath the house.

GOTDAMIT, he shouts. Hes shaking his hand one minute and knocking me down the next. He turns the sink on and sticks his hand in it. You didnt turn it off, he says.

I get up and rub my chin. Wheres the switch, I say.

He points his wet finger at me and says, Dont be a smartass.

I dont even know what that is.

He turns the sink off. Wheres your Mama, he says.

I dont say a thing.

He grabs me by my ear and starts dragging me through the house. Wheres your gotdam mother, he says.

Outside, I say.

He pulls me into their bedroom and shouts, DARSE.

OUTSIDE, I say.

He leads me through the front door and lets me go. Where, he says.

I grab the tarp and throw it back, but theres nobody there. Shit, I say. I drag the tarp all over the yard. THERES NO MAMA.

Thanksgiving

Idiot, Daddy says. His hands on his hips.

Im looking on both sides of the tarp. She was right here, I say.

He storms back inside. DARSE, he shouts.

Im looking under the house. Im looking up in the trees.

SHERWOOD, he shouts, and I run through the door. The fans blowing the black smoke away. I run through the house till he catches me. Wheres she, he says.

Dont know, I say, and he knocks me down.

And I get up, and he says, Wheres your Gramma.

Dont know, I say, and he knocks me down.

And I get up, and he says, Wheres Squirt.

Dont know, I say, and he knocks me down.

And I get up, and he says, Im gonna ask you one more time.

Its Tooth Fairy time. My left eyes closed. Im looking at him through my right eye when he says, Whered you take them.

And all of a sudden, I dont know why, I CANT REMEMBER, so I close my eye and say, I dont remember. Which is the truth.

I hear glass breaking, and I open my eye, and Daddys on the floor, and Mamas standing over him, holding a bottleneck.

She kicks Daddy in the head and says, Dont go hitting my baby.

But Daddys up like a tiger. He grabs Mama and throws her into the wall. She slides right down. I help her up. Her noses bleeding. Shes crying black tears.

Sherwood, she says. Darling. She looks at me. Go outside and play. She pats me on top of the head, and then she grabs Daddys bowling trophy and knocks him over the coffee table. Shes smiling. Go on, Sweetheart, she says.

I close the front door behind me. This is when Mama starts a-screaming. This is when the decoys start flying out the windows. Some of thems Squirts decoys. Some of thems mine. Glass breaking. Redheads and Buffleheads. Blue-winged Teals and Green-winged Teals. Ruddys and Pintails. Wood ducks and Mallards. Canvasbacks and Mergansers. Every window in the house.

— — —

39

Once upon a time, I played this game. Squirt helped. Not really. I saw this show with this cat and this rat.

Mama makes some pretty things. She paints these pictures. She cuts them out and hangs them in her classroom. She uses tacks and sticks them to her walls. These aint no normal tacks. Thesere GIANT JUMBO thumbtacks. I saw this once on a TV show.

This was way back long time ago when Squirt lived with me. Back when he was still wearing his diapers. I woke him up in the middle of the night. I piggybacked him into the living room and plopped him into Daddys chair.

Wheres the tree, he says.

What, I say.

Wheres the tree, he says.

Shut up, I say.

Every day when the bell rang, Id leave Miss Bingham and The Special Class and walk to Mamas room. Mama was drawing things. Mama was painting things. Mama was happy when she was at school. Every day, Id walk to Mamas room and take a box of tacks.

I piggybacked Squirt into the living room and plopped him into Daddys chair.

Wheres my present, he says.

Shut up, I say.

I dumped all the boxes on the floor. I started outside Mama and Daddys door. I crawled backwards into the living room. Box after box. Tack after tack. I made sure each was standing up straight. I turned the lights off. I turned my flashlight on that I take out to the blinds. One trillion tacks. The hallway sparkled with them shiny points. The floor looked like some kind of torture device.

Squirt says, This gonna be scary.

No, I say. I shine my flashlight on his face. This gonna be funny, I say. This gonna be the funniest thing you ever saw.

What do we do, he says.

What youre gonna do is this, I say. Youre gonna scream, I say. Youre gonna scream Bloody Murder.

When, he says.

When I tell you to, I say. I turn the flashlight off. I hide behind the chair. ok, I whisper.

What, he says.

scream, I whisper.

Now, he says.

now, I whisper.

scream, he goes.

No, I say. I whack him on top of the head with the flashlight. Scream Bloody Murder.

What does that mean, he says.

Scream like someones hacking you up with a ax, I say.

I dont want to play, he says. This gonna be scary.

Im sorry, I say and reach round and pinch the Holy Hell out of him.

This sets him off, and he cranks out a good one. thats it, I whisper and pinch him even harder, and he takes a deep breath and cranks out nother one. thats more like it, I whisper and dig in with my fingernails, and I cant imagine anybody screaming any louder even if they was being hacked up with a ax.

The bedroom door flies open. The knob sticking in the wall. Daddy comes storming into the hallway in his underwear, and I turn the flashlight on and tell Squirt, Watch this.

When Daddys foot finds the first tack, he bout goes through the roof, and then he comes down on the other foot, and back up he goes again just like that cat on that TV show, and hes hopping round like the floors on fire, and I cant take it anymore, so I say, Here, and I give Squirt the flashlight and fall on the floor and start rolling all over the place.

Daddys tap dancing with tacks, and then he falls down hard.

Woody, Squirt says.

Now Daddys got all them tacks on his back.

Woody, Squirt says.

Now Daddys lying on his side, pulling himself towards us. Just wait, he says over and over.

Woody, Squirt says.

Now Daddys bleeding, dragging himself cross the floor. when I get there, he whispers, Im gonna kill you.

And bout this time I stop laughing, and bout this time Squirt turns the flashlight off, and Im sitting there in the dark, thinking bout Daddy, all bloody, crawling cross the floor, reaching out to snatch us, and Im thinking bout poor Squirt who didnt want to do this anyway, whos sitting up in that chair by himself, and all I can think to do to save him is shout, RUN.

Im wandering round the yard, picking the ducks up. Im toting them to the truck and sitting them in the bed. One by one. Duck by duck. See, I say, I told you you could fly.

Whats going on over there. Its Mr Rockwell. Hes standing on his porch. Hes sorting his decoys. What is it, he says.

Thanksgiving, I say.

SHERWOOD. Someones shouting. Its Daddy. SHERWOOD.

Coming, I say. I run inside. Im holding a Bufflehead under my arm like a football. Im coming.

The houses dark. Theres no one in there. The back doors open. Theres holes in the windows where the ducks flew through. Theres a chair with all four legs sticking in the wall. The coffee tables broke. The TVs exploded. daddy, I whisper.

Someone grabs me by the neck and throws me up against the wall. Calling your Daddy, she says. Her lips smeared. Her eyes black.

Shes got me by the throat. This is all your fault, she says.

SHERWOOD, Daddy shouts. Hes out back.

She knocks my head back against the wall. She smiles. Ill get you for this, she says.

SHERWOOD.

She lets go and limps down the hallway.

IM COMING, I say and run out the door.

Hes on his hands and knees, looking underneath the house. Where you been, he says.

I found Mama, I say.

He stands up. He slaps his knees with his hands. Shithead, he says.

Yesir, I say.

You did this, he says. He stretches his arms wide. You did all this. You made this mess, and now youre gonna clean it up.

Clean it up, I say.

He steps towards me, and I step back.

DONT YOU DARE RUN, he says. YOU STAND YOUR GOTDAM GROUND. YOU TAKE WHATS COMING TO YOU.

Yesir, I say.

Listen to me, he says. I gotta get back to the shop. I gotta lock up. But Ill be back. Ill be right back. You hear me.

I hear you, I say.

And you know what youre gonna do, he says.

Nosir, I say. Which is the truth.

He shakes his head. We shoulda just drownt you at birth, he says. He takes a deep breath. Youre gonna fix this, he says. Youre gonna fix all this fore I get back.

Fore you get back, I say.

He points his finger at me. I mean it, he says. Find your Gramma. Find Squirt. Find the turkey. This is Thanksgiving, gotdamit.

Thanksgiving, I say.

He makes a fist, and I close my eye, and I keep it closed till I hear him breaking glass back inside. I stay out there till I hear the wrecker, till I cant hear it screaming down the road.

I peep my head through the back door. Everythings dark. I squint my eyes. mama, I whisper.

Everythings quiet. I can hear the dogs snoring underneath the house.

mama, I whisper. I tiptoe inside. mama. I gotta be careful. Theres glass all over the floor. The living room smells like Mama shouting. I can see Daddys broke Mamas bottles. I can see something shiny sitting on the bar. Its Daddys church key, and maybe for a second Im thinking bout tonight, and then Im running down the hall shouting, MAMA.

I stop outside. My doors open. My rooms dark. O Mama, I say. I can hear the pump, but I cant hear the gurgling.

I step inside, and theres the tank on the Chester drawers, and theres the four cans of motor oil.

The tanks filled right up to the brim. The oils a black blanket sitting on top of the water. I cant see the blue rocks on the bottom. I cant see my little fishes anywhere. I look all over the place. I look in the white castle where I would go and hide.

I grab my net and scoop them out. My zebras. My tigers. My neon tetras. I cant tell one from the other. Theyre just laying there on their sides in the tar.

I run into the bathroom and fill the sink. I run back and forth with my net. One by one. Fish by fish. I wash them off, but its too late.

I turn my light on in case I missed one, and there he is on the floor, halfway cross the room, Jack Dempsey. I can see the splash where he landed. I can see the oil he left behind. I can see the trail where he was trying to get underneath my bed, trying to get to my tunnel, trying to get to my secret passageway, and if he got that far, he could escape.

HOW FAR ARE WE
FROM THE WATER?

Sadness is fogging the back window, his tail wagging, his nose pressed against the pane.

"Shoo," she tells him. She takes off her sweater. "Shoo!" She is frowning. "We leave all these lights on?"

Both pole lamps on both sides of the love seat. The chandelier! The bare bulb above the kitchen sink. Even the back floodlights are on.

"We didn't, did we?" She looks behind her. "Ryne?" She walks back into the entry hall. "Where are you?" she says. The front door still open.

She pulls her key from the lock, steps onto the porch, and then she sees him, standing out in the yard, his hands in his jeans pockets. "Ryne?"

"You know what these are?" he says, nudging something in the tall grass with his boot.

She points. "I need to mow that."

"These," he says, kicking a large green bois d'arc ball onto the side-walk.

"They come off that old tree," she says.

"They're called horse apples."

"Is that right," she says, walking slowly down the steps. "Ryne?"

A cold front blew through earlier in the evening. It has rained. The bark on the bois d'arc is wet on the north side. The hanging Spanish moss in the live oak, soaked.

"Ryne," she says, "why don't you come on inside?" She reaches out her arm for him.

He looks up at her. He smiles. "You think it'd be all right?"

"Sure," she says. "Come on, now. We're letting all the bugs in."

He climbs the steps to the porch and walks slowly into the house.

She is standing out in the dark yard. Everything is too quiet now. There are no cicadas crying through the night. There are no bullfrogs from the bayou. No crickets. Is this it? she is thinking. Is this winter?

She is looking through the trees, down the long driveway to the levee. She is hoping to hear something in this silence. A car passing on the levee road. A small V of geese heading south. Anything.

"This is really a nice place you got here," he says. He is standing in the den at the picture window.

"What's that?" she says, stepping out of the utility room. "Must have been every light in the house on."

"I was saying, You got a really nice place. It's even got a great backyard."

She just looks at him. "Yeah," she says. "It's got . . . grass and everything."

"This y'all's basset?"

Sadness waddles over to the back door. He looks at Ryne. He stops his tail. He looks at her, very disappointed.

"Get on," she says. She kicks at the panes in the door. "Get on away from there!"

"Can I get you something to drink?" she says, walking into the kitchen. She opens the refrigerator. "Let's see what we got in here," she says. "We got beer. Three beers. Lone Star."

"A beer'll be fine," he says.

"Some Cokes. Some Sprites. Got some old chicken in here. Want some chicken? Wine coolers. Got some wine. You like wine?"

He turns from the window. "I'll just take a beer," he says.

"White wine," she says. "Pretty cheap white wine I'm afraid." A bottle of champagne. She looks up out of the refrigerator. "What do you need?"

"*A beer,*" he says.

"Thank you," he says.

"I'm going to have a little wine," she says, "if I can just get this bottle open."

"I see y'all got an airboat."

"What?" she says from the kitchen, opening and slamming drawers. "Where in the hell is that little thing?"

"*The boat,*" he says. He points with his beer.

"The swamp boat," she says. "We had it out back by the garage, and somebody came by one night and stole the big airplane propeller type thing, so we had to move it inside the fence."

"It ain't much good without one," he says.

"You like wine?" she says. She walks into the den to the love seat.

"Sure," he says. "I haven't had much of it." He is looking at the garage. The side door is open. A light is on over the workbench. He can see a red vise, a welding machine, a small bateau. He says, "Don't know if I've ever had any wine."

"Do you know anything about it?"

"A little," he says, his back to her. "Not a whole lot. You know, people down here don't drink a lot of wine. Don't know if I know anybody that drinks wine."

"You do now," she says. She sits on the love seat. "Ryne?"

"How far are we from the water?"

"Ryne?"

He turns and looks at her. "Yes?" he says.

"Why don't you just come on over here and sit down?" she says. "I mean, you don't have to if you don't want to."

"You think?" he says.

"Sure," she says. She pats the seat beside her. "Here."

"I don't know what to make of this," she says, swirling the wine in her glass. "Want a sip?"

"Why not," he says and knocks down about a shot of it.

"What do you think?" she says.

He looks at the glass and frowns. "Not much of a bite," he says. "Tastes like old water. Flat water. Tastes like slow river water."

"I'm just learning," she says. "This probably isn't that good. I think you can run into a bad bottle every now and then." She lifts the glass and looks at it.

"It isn't really white, is it?"

"Pardon me?" she says.

"The wine," he says.

"No," she says. She just looks at him. "No, it isn't."

"But red wine is really red."

"Yes," she says. "It is."

"Why is that?"

She is staring past him, out the window, into the yard.

"What is it?" he says. He turns in the love seat and follows her look. "What's the matter?"

Sadness is out there, deep in the yard, pointing toward the garage, his tail wagging.

"Nothing," she says. She turns, and her eyes catch the bootjack by the fireplace. "Thought I heard someone on the driveway."

"Want me to go check?"

"No," she says. "Wouldn't be anybody at this hour."

"So," he says. He sips his beer. "Where is he?"

"Who?"

"The man who takes that boat to the slough," he says. "If you don't mind my asking."

"No," she says. "Not at all." She says, "Gone."

"Gone?"

"We're divorced," she says.

"I'm sorry," he says. "I didn't know. I wasn't sure."

"Yeah," she says. "I would've told you. It's just that. . . . It's just that sometimes even *I* don't believe it."

"How long's it been?"

She is looking out the window again. "About a couple years," she says. "Somewhere in there." She is looking deep into the dark thicket, past the property line where even the floodlights will not go. "What is this? November? Two years, a couple months, and a week now. Something like that."

"I'm separated," he says, reading the label on his beer bottle.

"That's what you said," she says. "You said that you were."

"But we're getting a divorce," he says. "If that's what she wants. I mean, if that's what we decide on."

"It's hard," she says.

He looks at her. "Does it get any easier?"

"Not for a while," she tells him. "Not for a while." She shakes her head. "Listen," she says, "if you don't mind, could we change the subject?"

"I'm sorry," he says.

"No," she says. "It's all right."

"Really," he says, "we shouldn't be talking about this anyway. I shouldn't be."

"It just doesn't do any good, you know," she says. "It just doesn't." She catches herself in the middle of a yawn, covers her mouth with her hand. "Pardon me," she says.

"I'm keeping you up," he says.

"No," she says.

"You just run me off when you're ready."

"Don't worry," she says. She yawns again. "I'm sorry."

And then, he yawns.

They both laugh.

"It's catching," he says. "Have you ever thought about that?"

"What?"

"Yawning," he says. "Why we do it? Why *do* we yawn? How do we catch it from other people?"

"I don't know," she says. She is looking at the clock above the fireplace. It is getting late.

"Have you ever thought about why we don't catch yawns from TV?" he says. "I mean, they're real people in there, you know. And they yawn, and we don't. Why is that?"

"They probably aren't real yawns," she says. "They probably just acted-out yawns, the ones that aren't contagious."

"You think?" he says. "And even talking on the telephone. You can be just talking to somebody on the telephone, and you can't see their eyes start to water, and you can't see their mouth wide open. You can just *hear* them, and it makes you yawn."

"Is that right," she says.

"I don't know when," he says, "but I know for certain that I once caught a yawn from a dog."

"I need some more wine," she says. She stands and walks into the kitchen. "Can I get you another beer?"

"If you don't mind," he says, leaning back in the love seat. He is smiling.

He hears her laughing in the kitchen. "What?" he says.

"Nothing," she says. She carries a beer out to him, places it on the coffee table. She looks at him. She gives him a kind smile, shakes her head, and walks back into the kitchen.

"Was that stupid or what?" he says loud enough for her to hear him.

"What?" she says.

He picks up his beer. "Talking about yawning."

He hears her laughing. "No," she says. She sticks her head around the corner. "No, I think it's . . . interesting. Let me get my wine."

He places his beer back on the coaster. He looks out the window and frowns. "I guess it was pretty stupid," he says to himself. "Who's that?"

"Who!" she says, walking quickly out of the kitchen.

The back door opens.

"That," he says.

"Mason!" she says.

But Mason has not stopped walking toward her. He has not even closed the back door. Sadness peeps his head around the corner. "Mason," she says, "Goddamnit!" She points at Ryne. "I've got . . . company."

Mason takes her by that hand and heads for the back of the house.

Ryne stands and looks confused.

"Excuse us," Mason tells him, pulling her gently into the back hallway.

"Goddamnit, Mason!" she says. She is walking behind him. She is being pulled along. She is not exactly resisting. "I have a guest in there!"

Without stopping, Mason points at the many pictures on the walls of the hallway. Family pictures. Her mother, her father. Donnie and Debbie. The nieces, the nephews. All smiling. "There we are," he says. "Happy."

"Don't do this," she says.

When they reach the dark bedroom, she stops, and he lets go of her hand and crawls onto the far side of the bed. He pats the comforter beside him. "Come here," he says.

"We ain't doing this again," she says. She stomps her foot. "God-damnit!" She points through the wall. "I got a *date* in there!"

He reaches up with his finger and hooks one of her belt loops and pulls her slowly down onto the bed with him.

She sets her glass of wine on the night table. "This is it!" she says. "You hear me?"

He takes her softly by the shoulders and lays her down next to him.

"Just for a second, now," she says. "I got to get back."

He slides his left leg over her. He nestles up next to her. He rests his head on her breast. "Hold me," he whispers.

"Goddamnit, Mason."

He reaches up with his left hand and finds her face, her mouth. He carefully closes her lips with his fingers. "Shhh," he tells her. He places his finger on her lips. "Shhh," he says.

The house is quiet. She is listening for Ryne. She is listening for the sound of the front door opening, listening for the sound of his truck starting, the sound of his tires on the oyster-shell driveway.

"Tell me," he says.

"What?" she says.

"Tell me everything's gonna be all right."

She places her hand on the side of his face. "Mason," she whispers.

"Tell me."

"Everything's gonna be all right," she says.

She feels something large land at their feet. "Did you leave the door open?" she says. "Did you let the dog in?" She lifts her head and looks down, and there he is, in silhouette, Ryne, slumped over, sitting at the foot of the bed.

"Tell me," he says.

WHEN THE GODS WANT
TO PUNISH YOU

Watch out, you might get what you're after.

Talking Heads
Stop Making Sense

"When the gods want to punish you," I tell him, "they answer your prayers."

"No shit," Donnie says. He's sitting at the bar between Debbie and Madison.

I'm standing in the kitchen, salting his glass.

"More lime this time," Madison says. She hands me her glass.

Donnie points to his. "More tequila," he says.

Debbie isn't drinking. She's pregnant.

Cazadores
Corazón
Don Julio
Herradura
Patrón
Porfidio

I hand him his drink.

"You know," he says, "I always wanted to be a fireman."

"Dear god," Madison says. She reaches for her glass. "Hurry."

Debbie hides her face in her hands.

"No," Donnie says, "I'm serious."

"We know," Debbie says through her fingers.

"Ever since I was a little kid."

Madison mouths the words, "Fire engine."

"I even had this little fire engine," he says. "Most little kids had little race cars, but I had a fire engine!"

"Was it red?" Madison says.

"It *was* red!" Donnie says. He looks at her. He's holding his head in his left hand, and then he's holding his head in his right hand. "It wasn't a toy," he says. "I mean, you could climb into it. It had pedals and everything. You know what I'm talking about?"

"We know," Debbie says. She lowers her hands and smiles at him.

"Tell us about the bell," Madison says.

"You saw it!" Donnie says.

"No," Madison says.

"Tell me the truth," Donnie says. "Did you ever see it?"

"No," Madison says, "I'm sorry."

"It had this little bell," he says. "Hell, I used to pedal that fire engine up and down our street, ringing that goddamn bell like crazy. Up and down the street. Back and forth." Donnie's pulling this invisible cord on this invisible bell. *"Ding ding ding ding ding ding ding,"* he goes. "All goddamn day."

"You're lucky somebody didn't shoot you," I tell him.

"Terry," Madison says.

"Can't you just picture it!" I say. "Some little maniacal bastard riding up and down the street, dawn to dusk, ringing this goddamned fire engine bell!"

"It wasn't *that* loud," Donnie says.

"Children!" I say.

"Terry," Madison says.

"Aren't children great!"

"Terrence."

"Don't get me started on children!" I say. "I mean, what cretins would ever *want* to have children unless they had guns to their. . . ."

"I think Debbie needs another drink," Madison says.

I throw Madison a stupid look and say, "Debbie's not drinking! She's . . . !"

"Let's just say there's a field," Donnie says. "It's nighttime."

"I need another Coke," Debbie says. "Please."

"The field is dark because the sun has gone down," he says. "It's about knee-deep in these black weeds."

"Black weeds?" Madison says.

"I told you!" he says. "It's dark!"

"Nighttime," she says.

"Anyway," he says, "in the middle of this black field, there's a small red fire."

"Call the fire department!" Madison says. She picks up the telephone receiver.

"That's right!" Donnie says. "I rush to the field with my bucket of water and put the fire out."

Debbie applauds.

"What could be more perfect than that?" Donnie says.

Madison finishes her drink. "It's not always that easy, is it?"

"That's not the point," he says. "The point is. . . . Anyway, that's what I used to dream about when I was a kid."

"When I was a kid," I tell him, "I used to dream about setting those fires."

"Let's just say your house is on fire," Donnie says.

"Call the fire department!" Madison says. She picks up the receiver.

"Our house?" I ask him.

"Somebody's house is on fire," he says.

"What's their name?" Madison says. "Maybe we should call them."

"Who?" he says.

"The people in the burning house," she says.

Donnie throws his hands in the air. "Help, help," he says, "our house is on fire!"

Debbie's laughing.

"Call the fire department!" Madison says. She hands Donnie the receiver and starts dialing 911.

"Don't do that!" he says. He reaches and hangs up the phone. "Let's just say the fireman gets the call, slides down his pole, jumps in his truck, and he's there. The house is consumed in flames."

"With flames," Madison says.

"He jumps out of his truck, hooks his hose to the hydrant, and starts spraying water on the house."

"A simian could do it," I tell him.

"Unless somebody's in there," Madison says. "Unless somebody's in the house."

"That's my point!" Donnie says. "Let's just say there's a baby in the house."

"Christ, Donnie!" Debbie says.

"Don't worry, Sweetie," he says. He reaches and kisses her cheek. "I'm gonna save it!"

I down my drink. "Chihuahuas," I tell him.

"Chihuahuas?" he says.

"Why don't we sprinkle in some Chihuahuas?" I say. I look at Madison. "I've never liked Chihuahuas."

"They wrap this wet blanket around me, and I run into this burning house."

"The way their skin starts to twitch," I say, "just before they bite you. Don't get me started on Chihuahuas!"

Donnie looks at me. *"I'm saving this baby if you don't mind."*

"Please," I say, "the house is collapsing all around you."

"That's my point!" he says. He hands me his glass. "We're all gonna die, and what better way to go than trying to save a baby?"

"Come here, Sweetheart," Debbie says. She puts her arms around him and kisses him. "I love you."

"Hurry," I tell him, "before those fucking Chihuahuas follow you out!"

"Anyway," Donnie says, "you're outside, throwing water on the house. It's consumed with flames."

"*By* flames," Madison says.

"The fire has spread across the roof. You got there as fast as you could, but it's fully involved. It's too late. The house is gonna burn right down to the foundation, and there's not a goddamn thing you can do about it. I mean, every rafter, every joist, two-by-four, two-by-twelve—it doesn't matter—every goddamn piece of furniture burned until there's nothing left but two white commodes sticking up out of the ashes."

I hand him his drink.

"Except that you're doing *something*," he says. "You're *trying* to save it. You're out there all night, throwing water on it, long past the point when you know that it's lost. You're not like the neighbors, standing in their robes, standing in their yards, staring at the flames, their hands in their pockets."

"Aren't neighbors great!" I tell him. "Don't get me started on neighbors!"

"And when it's all over," he says, "no fire, no flames, when all that's left of their house is just hissing—let's just say it's dawn—the people stumble over in their pajamas, crying, hugging each other, and they thank you. They thank you for doing *something*. They thank you for at least *trying*."

"A dead soldier!" I tell them. I hold up the bottle of liqueur.

"Road trip!" Donnie says. He pours himself off of his stool.

"It's way too late for that now," Debbie says. She keeps him from falling.

"Not to worry," I say. "We'll have to improvise. Besides, too much liqueur ruins the margarita."

"No chance of that now," Madison says.

I collect the glasses. "Tell them," I say.

Debbie looks at Donnie. "Do I know about this?" she says.

"Tell them about the refinery," I say. "Tell them about the end of the world."

"How do *you* know about the refinery?" Debbie says.

"He worked out there," Donnie says.

"I put my way through school out there."

"In the summers," Madison says.

"I spent one summer out there painting curbs," I tell them. "All day long. From 7:00 in the morning until 5:00 in the afternoon. From May until September. Crawling backwards on my hands and knees through the heat of the summer for miles and miles and miles."

Donnie's laughing. "College boy," he says.

"I mean, once you've painted about five miles of curb," I say, "you know every fucking thing you need to know."

I hand him his drink. "How is it?" I ask him. "The new recipe?"

He sips it and frowns. "Nasty," he says.

"Your supervisor, your foreman, coming out every now and then to check on you. He'd sit there in his golf cart and watch you. He'd bring a calendar with him, and he'd say, 'Sure is hot!' He'd say, 'Let's see: three and a half more months, fifteen more weeks, seventy-five more days!' And then he'd just drive off. He'd just drive off and shout over his shoulder, 'Don't get too hot, now!'"

"College boys!" Donnie says. "Most of the guys out there didn't finish high school. And we get these college boys for two or three months out of the year, and we're thinking one year from now, maybe two, these boys'll be wearing ties. They'll have good jobs—air-conditioned. They'll be bankers and doctors and lawyers."

"Tell them about the buildings," I say. "The way they're named."

Donnie smiles. "They're not called what you'd think," he says, "'The Paint Shop' and 'The Welding Shop' and 'The Carpenter Shop.' They're called, 'A Building' and 'B Building' and 'C Building.'"

"Tell them why," I say.

"Christ," Madison says, "you'd better fix me another drink! This is beginning to sound like a GRE question!"

"If anything ever happens," Donnie says, "if there's a fire or a big explosion, you're supposed to report to *your* building. Aikman would go to 'A Building.' Brady would go to 'B Building.' Culpepper would go to 'C Building.'"

"I knew it," Madison says. *"Hurry."*

"For what purpose?" Debbie says.

"For a body count," I say. I hand Madison her drink.

"So they'll know who's dead," Donnie says. "So they'll know who's still out there."

"But it's a joke, right?" I ask him. "They're not serious?"

"They're serious," Donnie says.

"Tell me it's a joke," I say. "You're working out there, you're hard at work, you're only about half paying attention to what you're doing, and you hear this roar, this explosion, and the concussion knocks you to the ground, and you look up, and everybody's running for the fence."

"You'd feel the concussion first," he says.

"I mean, you've got welders and pipe fitters, carpenters and engineers, all running for the fence. Because when that refinery goes, it's going to take the Gulf Coast with it."

Donnie's laughing. "So everybody's hauling ass for the fence," he says. "And they don't even climb it. . . ."

"You don't have time to climb it!"

"You got about five thousand men jumping on a fence at once," he says, "and their weight just carries it over."

"And then it's the mad dash for the water!"

"And then it's the Mile Mad Dash for the Bay," he says, "with the whole fucking world blowing up behind you!"

"'A Building,' my ass!"

"You don't slow down," he says. "You don't even stop when you hit the water. You just keep running until you can't anymore, until it gets too deep to run."

"All you can see," he says, "all around you, are these hard hats just above the surface. White for painters. Green for welders. Yellow, electricians. Red, firefighters. All of you up to your safety glasses in the salt water."

"As long as I can remember," Donnie says, "my old man was a firefighter. He worked at just about every refinery up and down the Channel."

I hold up the bottle of Herradura. "We have enough for one more," I tell them.

"Is that it?" Madison says.

"Then we have to get going," Debbie says. She puts her arm around Donnie.

"I can remember my old man bringing these things home," he says. "A helmet, a charred fire ax, a Dalmatian puppy."

"I've been meaning to talk to you about those dogs," I tell him. "You really ought to bathe them every now and then. You know, spray them down. Scrub some of that goddamned soot off of them."

"I always wanted to be a fireman," Donnie says, "and because he wound up at the refinery, I started out there. I painted hydrants for the first two years. Every goddamn day!"

"*El fin!*" I tell them and hand them their drinks.

"*El fin!*" Madison says, and we toast the end.

"We need to go soon," Debbie says.

"Do you know how many hydrants we got out there?" he says. "It's the biggest fucking refinery in this hemisphere!"

"Good for you," Madison says. She touches her glass to his. "You're starting at the top."

"That's what I tell him," Debbie says.

"That's my point!" Donnie says. "It *is* the biggest. It *is* the best. It *is* the most efficient."

"Your father would be proud of you," Debbie says.

"That's just it!" Donnie says. "It's too clean. It's too efficient. It's too safe."

"Donnie," Debbie says.

"Nothing ever happens," he says. "No alarms. No explosions. No fires."

"When the gods want to punish you," I tell him.

"No shit," he says. "So we just sit around all day and play with our hoses."

"So *that's* what's going on in those stations!" I say.

Donnie beckons me to come closer. He drapes an arm around Debbie and Madison. We huddle together. He whispers, "I have this dream about setting a fire."

"Donnie," Debbie says. She tries to pull away.

He pulls her back. "So we'd have something to do," he says.

"A little one?" Madison says.

Donnie grins. "No," he whispers. "A big one! A real big one!"

"Donnie!" Debbie says.

"Out at the refinery," he says. "The biggest fucking fire in the history of the world!"

I look at Madison. Madison looks at me.

"We sit around at lunch and talk about it," he says.

"We need to go," Debbie says.

"But then," Madison says. She pulls away from the huddle. "But then, you'd be good enough to put it out. You'd be good enough to save us."

"Of course!" Donnie says. "That's what firefighters do! They fight fires!"

"The entire refinery?" Madison says.

Donnie downs his drink. "Why not?" he says. "We'd make sure of it. We know all the hot spots."

"You'd be killed," Madison says.

"Good," he says. "Good."

Debbie grabs his arm and says, "Time to go."

"Better to die sprinting into fire than to die drooling in bed!"

"Go to the study," I tell Madison, "before it's too late!"

She spills herself off of her stool.

"Collect all of my students' assignments!"

"Why?" she says.

"Collect all of your students' assignments!"

She's smiling.

"Donnie!" I say.

"Yes sir!" he says. He salutes.

"Find the water hose!"

"Will do!" he says. He walks out back.

"Debbie!" I say.

She's frowning.

"Listen, Debbie," I say, "you are crucial to the implementation. Here are the matches. Go into the garage and find the barbecue pit. Bring us the lighter fluid, please."

She's just looking at me.

"Hurry," I tell her, "there's not a second to lose!"

Donnie's left the back door open. I walk out into the yard. "How are we doing out here!" I say.

"I found the hose!" he says from somewhere in the darkness.

"Good!" I tell him. "Take it around front!"

There's a wheelbarrow leaning up against the back fence. I grab it and start pushing it toward the house.

"Everything?" Madison shouts from the study.

"Everything!" I tell her. I'm having trouble getting the wheelbarrow through the back door. "Every goddamned thing!" I tell her. "Notebooks, note cards, rough drafts, revisions, diaries, journals, outlines, footnotes, endnotes, bibliographies, research papers, essays, personal, expository, comparison/contrast, how-to. . . ." I'm ramming the wheelbarrow into the door frame. "How-to-get-a-wheelbarrow-inside-your-wheel-house!" I'm backing up and getting a good run at it.

Debbie's standing in the middle of the den. She's holding the lighter fluid in one hand, the matches in the other. She's looking at me like she's never seen anything like this in her whole fucking life. "Madison," she says, "you'd better come in here!"

"Students!" I say.

Madison runs into the den. "Terry!" she shouts.

"Aren't students great!" I say.

"Terrence," she says. She's blocking the doorway with her body. "We don't need the wheelbarrow in the house."

"Those goddamned students!" I say.

"I know," she says.

I'm standing in the middle of the yard, holding the wheelbarrow, preparing for another run at it as soon as she steps out of the way. "If it weren't for the students," I tell her, "teaching would be great!"

"I know," she says. "Let me have the wheelbarrow."

"Don't get me started on students!"

I'm stretched out on the sofa, listening to the stereo. I'm watching the angels dance, and I don't know why but I'm thinking about Electric Football.

Madison's in the kitchen preparing these muffins. She's in the kitchen preparing these Pillsbury blueberry muffins. She has this theory.

The muffins aren't for breakfast. It's 3:47.

She has this theory that if she can attach something *cute* like muffins to something *ugly* like tequila she won't get sick.

"Good luck!" I shout over the stereo.

She has this theory that if she *completely* fills her stomach with these warm, sweet, moist Pillsbury blueberry muffins that they will in effect soak up all of the tequila, and she won't vomit.

"Good luck!" I shout. I'm in the den, watching the angels, listening to the Talking Heads.

The amplifier's set at 8.7. It's never been above 9. I remember reading a warning somewhere, something about the speakers, something about losing structural integrity somewhere around 10.

Every now and then, in between songs, I'll shout out, "MUFFINS," and Madison will walk into the den and kiss me on the forehead and say, "Why don't you turn that thing down!"

We had this game when we were kids. It was called Electric Football. There was this metallic board about the size of a desk top. It was green. It was the football field. It had yard markers and everything.

There were two teams of football players. Every position. Plastic. Miniature, of course. Maybe each player was two inches tall. It didn't matter which position you played—you were two inches tall!

Each player stood on his own little stand, a pedestal, kind of like on a plastic army man except that each of these stands stood on its own little feet—little feelers—like the legs of a centipede.

The two kids flipped a coin to decide which team would start on offense. They arranged their players on the line of scrimmage. Centers, guards, tackles.

The football was a wedge of felt you stuck under the arm of your quarterback. He was the player with his other arm sticking straight out in front of him. His legs frozen in the midst of a sprint.

This game, this football game, was unlike any other because it was indeed *electric*. The board, the big green playing field, had a cord. One of you just plugged it into the wall.

There was a switch on the cord, and the kid on offense flipped that switch when he was ready. My little brother had these absurd signals. "20 Blue!" he would shout. "20 Blue! 14 92! 17 76! 18 12! 20 Blue! 18 36! 18 61! 18 98! 20 Blue! 19 14! 19 39! 19 41!" before he would ever say, "Hike!" and flip the switch. "20 Blue!" he would shout. "20 Blue!" until you finally had to reach over and slap the shit out of him.

"Hike!" he would finally say, and he would flip the switch, and the play would start. The entire board, the entire playing surface, the entire football field would start to vibrate and hum, and all of the players, offensive and defensive, would spring into motion.

The play was not over, the quarterback not down, until he was *touched* by a player on the opposing team. The ball was not dead until one of the defensive players *bumped* into your quarterback.

You could design your plays. You could set up elaborate end runs with pulling guards, intricate sweeping reverses, wicked draws. But what made Electric Football fascinating was that you could not predict what your players would do—how they would move, where they would go.

You spent minutes meticulously lining them up, pointing them in the right direction, placing them in their proper positions, and then you flipped the switch, the whistle blew, and it became the Bedlam Bowl.

Sometimes, well-intentioned, seemingly competent centers quickly pivoted and began blocking the quarterback.

Sometimes, guards and tackles hooked elbows and began dancing over a hash mark.

Sometimes, sure-handed, fleet-footed wide receivers sprinted directly off the field and spent the duration of the play butting their heads against the bleachers.

Sometimes, cunning, calculating, carnivorous linebackers pirouetted at midfield.

Sometimes, my league leader in yardage, my Heisman trophy winner, my number one draft pick, my star running back spent five, ten, fifteen minutes running around in circles, around and around, looking for the ball, looking for the play.

And it never failed—my quarterback, my Bradshaw, Staubach, my Montana, received the snap, faded back and back, faster and faster, until he was running for the wrong end zone where he bounced off of the goal post and started gyrating, slowly at first and then more rapidly, faster and faster, until he dropped the ball.

Down in one end zone, next to the scoreboard, there was a dial that regulated the vibration of the board.

After the two of you had been sitting there watching the same play for thirty minutes, forty-five minutes, and the quarterback still wasn't tackled—the quarterback wasn't even *close* to being tackled (I mean, there wasn't a defensive player within the same zip code, the same county, the same fucking state)—one of you simply turned the dial to increase the intensity of the game. One of you simply intensified the search for the ball.

The owner's manual recommended a dial setting of 3 for optimal game conditions. But you could turn the dial to 6 and increase the vibration of the board. You could turn the dial to 6 and increase the desire of each player.

At the setting of 6, both offensive and defensive players sprint frantically about the field, running in and out of bounds. At the setting of 6, the players, in a panic, spin uncontrollably, their hands in the air. They have forgotten the rules. They can remember the search, but they cannot remember the object of the search.

At the setting of 9, the entire world is shaking. Veteran tight ends fall to their faces. Acrobatic cornerbacks complete full gainers. Safeties fly through the uprights into the stands. Nose tackles lie on their backs in convulsions. The players have long since forgotten the search.

I'm stretched out on the sofa, listening to the stereo, watching the angels dance.

Madison collects angels. She collects crystal angels, pewter angels, angels made of porcelain, angels made of stone. She collects kissing angels, some with halos, most with wings.

They are dancing around on the top shelf between the large speakers. They are fluttering about, brushing their wings against one another. Their halos cocked at precarious angles. The kissing angels are promiscuous. They are switching partners. They peck, and then they flit and flirt, and then they pucker for someone new.

"Angels!" I shout toward the kitchen.

"What!" she says.

"Aren't angels great!" I shout.

"I can't hear you!" she says.

"Don't get me started on angels!"

"Why don't you turn that damned thing down!" she says.

I reach and turn the dial to 9.

The angels, wing tip to wing tip, have huddled together now. They are all facing the same direction. The whole herd of them shuffles slowly toward the edge of the shelf.

Did I hear it or feel it? Without knowing how, I'm off the sofa on my hands and knees on the floor. The stove! "Madison!" I shout over the music. I get to my feet, turn off the stereo, and she's standing right in front of me. "Are you okay?" I ask her, and without thinking, we're holding each other's hands.

"What was that?" she says.

I'm thinking that it was a nightjar, a sea gull, a screech owl flying through the night. The light's on in the den. I'm thinking that an owl flew into the bay window.

"It's all right," I tell her. "Let me go check." I open the back door.

"Be careful," she says.

I'm thinking Barn, Barred, Great Horned Owl. I'm thinking I can pick it up, pet it, hold it for a minute, make sure its head's looking in the right direction, climb up on the roof, and then toss it back into the night.

"The window shook!" she says.

"Why don't you go get the flashlight," I tell her.

I step out into the dark and notice, one by one, lights coming on in the neighborhood.

I'm looking around on the ground, trying to figure out where I'd be if I were a dazed owl, trying to figure out how far most owls bounce.

This time, I both hear it *and* feel it. "Goddamn!" I say. I find myself sitting on the ground.

"Terry!" Madison shouts. She runs out of the back door. "Terry!" She's looking for me with the flashlight.

"Over here!" I say.

"Are you all right?" she says. She shines the flashlight in my face.

"Help me up," I say.

"What was that?" she says.

"An explosion," I say. "Somewhere out there."

I look at Madison. Madison looks at me. We start smiling.

"Call him," I tell her.

"I will not!" she says. "They're in bed by now!"

"Call him," I tell her. "I'll bet he's getting ready. I'll bet he's about to leave."

"Is it the refinery?" she says.

"I don't know," I say. "I'm not sure." She hands me the flashlight. "Call him."

Madison's grinning. *"This is your idea,"* she says and walks back inside.

I climb up on the air conditioner, onto the fence, into the mimosa. I drop down onto the roof. I crawl up to the peak and stand. "Where are you?" I say.

I shine the flashlight toward South America, the Gulf of Mexico, Galveston Island, the bay. "That's south," I say. I move the beam slowly up the Ship Channel. Du Pont. Phillips. Shell. Ethyl. Arco. Exxon. No fire.

I'm thinking of him putting his boots on the wrong feet. I'm thinking of him kissing Debbie goodbye and then hobbling hurriedly out of his house. I'm thinking of him falling off of the fire truck, rolling back home all the way down the road.

I'm standing up on top of the roof. I'm shouting, "Donnie!" I'm laughing. I'm shouting at the tops of my lungs, *"Donnie, you'd better wake your ass up!"*

Madison runs out into the dark. "What is it?" she says. "What's the matter?"

I'm laughing so hard I can barely stand up.

"Where are you?" she says.

"Up here!" I tell her.

"Goddamnit, Terry!" she says. "Get down from there! You're going to fall and break your goddamned neck!"

I take a deep breath, fill my lungs with the night air, tilt my head back, and shout at every fire in the sky, "D O N N I E !"

"To the Bat Poles!" I shout, sliding down the mimosa. I run around the corner of the house. "Phasers on stun!"

She catches me. "Shhh!" she says. "You'll wake the neighbors!"

I look around the neighborhood. There's a light on in every house. "Everyone's awake!" I tell her.

She places her hand over my mouth.

"The truck," I whisper.

"Let me get my purse," she says and runs inside.

I climb up on the picnic table and shout in the direction of Donnie's house, "Call the fire department!"

"I'm coming!" she says. "Would you shut up!"

"Yeah, shut the fuck up!" someone says from across the fence.

Madison's standing at the back door, jingling her keys up over her head.

"Shotgun!"

I roll down the window. "D O N N I E !" I shout into the night.

Madison grabs me by the belt and pulls me back inside. "Is your door locked?" she says. "Where are we going?"

I turn on the flashlight and point through the windshield. "That way," I tell her.

"Turn that off!" she says. "I can't see a thing!"

I shine the flashlight through my window. "North," I tell her.

"North?" she says. "There's nothing north!"

"There most certainly is!" I tell her. "Mobay. Mobay is north. Chevron. Chevron is north. And that other big one in Mont Belvieu. The one that's on the salt dome. The one that's always blowing up."

"I hope you know what you're talking about," she says.

We cross the creek on Main Street. We head north, away from the bay. We leave the dead town behind us, the boarded windows, the closed shops, the empty stores.

We can see the interstate in the distance, and we can see the bright lights of the shopping mall pulsing like the town's new heart.

"Malls!" I say.

The vast parking lot vacant. There are two vehicles parked side by side, nose to tail. Security guards.

I shine the flashlight on the two of them. "Aren't malls great!" I say.

"Where are we going?" she says.

"They build a shopping mall," I tell her. "They build a mall, and they run all of the mom-and-pop shops out of business. They suck the living blood out of a town."

"Terrence," she says.

"Don't get me started on shopping malls!" I say.

We leave the lights of the interstate behind us, the stations supplied with gasoline by the refineries up and down the Channel. The mall is only a small dome of light in the distance.

Madison drives on through the early morning into the dark green miles of rice country.

"Terry," she says, *"we're out in the middle of nowhere."*

"This is a short cut," I tell her.

"A short cut," she says. She shakes her head.

I point the flashlight to the northeast. "It should be over there somewhere."

"Should be," she says. *"Somewhere."*

"Stop the truck," I tell her. "Let me get out and check."

"Let's go home," she says. *"This isn't even Donnie's fire."*

She stops the truck. I open the door and hop out. "But he'll be called," I tell her. "It's a big one, and he'll be called to help."

The concussion knocks me back against the truck. The next explosion is so much louder because we're so much closer, because there are no houses, because there are no trees.

An enormous fireball lights up the sky.

"Goddamn!" I shout. I'm pointing. *"Did you see that!"* I run around to the back of the truck. *"Hurry,"* I tell her, *"or we'll miss it!"*

"Get in!" she says.

I climb over the tailgate and walk up the bed to the cab. "I'm in!" I tell her. "Let's go!"

"At least, close your door!" she says.

"It'll close!" I tell her. "Just gun it!"

"Hang on!" she shouts. She stamps the gas pedal, the truck jumps forward, the door slams shut, and I fall on my butt in the bed.

I get to my feet and stand behind the cab.

We're flying up Main Street, past acres and acres of rice fields. The dark green on both sides as far as I can see. We cross a service road every mile down the street. The fields exactly one mile square.

The horizon is ablaze. Another fireball shoots into the sky. The refinery is on the highway, still some ten miles away.

I lean around and shout into the driver's window, "Take a right at the next road! I can see it!"

She takes the corner too quickly, slides off of the road, and almost loses me. "W H O O E E !" I shout.

I lean around again and shout against the wind, "One for left! Two for right!" I demonstrate. I strike the top of the cab like I'm playing a kettledrum. "Left!" I shout.

"Got it!" she says.

I'm looking over the cab at the burning horizon. "D O N N I E !" I shout. "Ready or not, here we come!"

We're flying down oyster-shell service roads. I look through the back window, and we're going seventy-five miles per hour. Madison's turn indicator is still flashing. I love this woman! Behind us, billowing clouds of white dust fan out over the fields.

Madison's turned on the stereo. "Louder?" she shouts.

"Louder!" I tell her.

Talking Heads shout out of the window.

I'm standing behind her, my arms stretched out over the cab, singing "Psycho Killer" at the tops of my lungs into the early morning. There are so many dead bugs on my glasses I can't see anything clearly. The road is just a blurry white strip beyond the headlights.

"Swamp" is on now.

We're zigging down service roads, zagging toward the horizon. "Left!" I shout, a rice field later, "Right!" North for a mile, and then for a mile, east.

I'm playing the bongos in "Slippery People" on top of the cab until my fingers are stinging.

A pause. The crowd applauds. And then, the drums. And then, "Watch out, you might get what you're after."

"The muffins!" she shouts, and all of a sudden, the truck is sliding sideways down the road, and directly between beats, my drum is gone, and I am tossed, hurled, ejected, launched.

I'm airborne, soaring high over the dark fields, my arms straight out in front of me just like Superman—not this latest color asswipe—just like the original black-and-white Superman, flying with both arms sticking out in front of me—not like Mighty Mouse who always had one arm cocked back to punch some fucking cat. "Up, up, and away!" I shout. What was the actor's name, the one who played the first Superman, the one who shot himself to death—not quite faster than a speeding bullet? What was the actor's name, the one who played the second Superman, the one who fell and broke his neck attempting one last jump—not quite able to leap tall buildings in a single bound?

Higher and higher into the sky I fly. Far down below, I can see the light brown rice canals, the light green levees.

Muffins?

I look over my shoulder, and the truck is only a pair of taillights disappearing into the dust.

"Muffins!" I shout out in front of me.

Behind me, the horizon is on fire. I can see the flames. I'm shouting, "Aren't muffins great!"

Higher and higher into the sky I fly—until I can see flames on both horizons, until I can see two fires—up and up to that point where I just stop, still, motionless for a moment, where I feel the first slight tug at my little toe, and before I go, I shout, "Don't get me started on muffins!"

SHOOTING STARS

Summer, past midnight. The windows are open. A scratch at the screen.

"Listen," I whisper, shake her softly by the shoulder. "Sweetheart, it's time."

"Really?" she says. She's suddenly awake. She sits up in bed. "Well then, let's go!"

The scratching becomes a soft rapping on the wooden screen frame. I hurry over. Any second it will wake our mother. I can see him outside, standing there in his jeans, slumped, no shirt, holding a rifle. "We're coming," I whisper. It must be a clear night.

I help her on with her slippers. Little rabbits Mamma made of cloth. The head at her toes, a cotton nose. The long ears stick out on both sides of the shoe.

I unlatch the screen, lift and set her on the sill. He has already propped his rifle against the house, and when I push the bottom of the rusty screen out, he reaches in and takes her.

"Careful," I tell him.

She looks over her shoulder, frowning. She reaches back for me.

"*My* . . . ," she says too loudly, and they are gone hand in hand into the darkness.

I grab her sock filled with pennies from the night stand and crawl backwards through the window, bumping the screen open with my bottom.

They are to the road by now, so I run after them, in my pajamas, barefooted through the night.

No one is awake at this hour. No porch lights. There is no moon.

Deep in the Thicket, there are few places, if any sometimes, to see the sky. The road is the only paved passageway through this wood. There are places where the trees grow together overhead to form a dark tunnel for miles.

But here, on both sides, there are loblolly pines, high, a good strip of sky. This is where I find them. He, with his back turned, loading the rifle. She, off to one side.

It has always amazed me how the blacktop holds its heat through the night. Impossible to cross barefooted at noon. It is warm now under my feet, soporific. On chilly nights, after heavy rains, the animals of the Thicket hop, slither, crawl out of the cold marshes onto this road, stretch out on it, dry, warm as a mother's side, and sleep until a car comes along.

She beckons with her hand. It means, "Hurry." Little prints of sleeping rabbits on her pajamas. Little sister.

She takes the sock of coins and hands it to the quiet one. She is wide-awake now, so proud of herself.

He tucks the rifle under his arm, empties the sock into his palm and shakes that hand up and down to hear the sound of the coins in the dark. He pours them into his pocket, lifts the rifle above his head and points it at the sky.

Now it is my turn as intermediary to pick her up and show her the stars.

She is to select one, not a big star because it would not be fair. I am to tell the quiet one which star she has chosen. He will aim his rifle, take time aiming, seconds, minutes, and then shoot that burning orb from the sky. It will fall, plummet, race straight down to the earth, Western Hemisphere, North America, East Texas, Big Thicket, strike the asphalt some half mile away, explode (not loudly, for it is a tiny star) and then burn itself out in the darkness.

"Aww," she will say. This is what pains me. She will look so sad. She will start running down the blacktop for the fallen star which is now just a tiny fire disappearing in the distance. She will not get there in time.

"Aww," she will say like the day she held her Easter chick in her hands and watched it die.

How can I tell her about these things? How can I tell her it is not true when she wants to believe so badly? How can I tell her that what he loads and fires, the projectile, is a wee wooden arrow, kitchen match, three inches long, propelled by a small metal sphere, pushed down the barrel high in the sky up to that point where something in the earth calls it back—that it then falls, plunges, red head first, white-eyed, quite a ways, so that when it strikes the pavement, it strikes and burns a dying fire down the dark road?

One of her slippers falls to the blacktop. "I'll get it," I tell her, stoop and grab the rabbit by the ears.

We are both staring straight up out of the Thicket. I raise my hand to show her. . . . The night is a black beast, a winged thing, with a thousand eyes.

Will I have the time to one day tell her that this star, a star we see one night, went out, is dead, died a long time ago—there is no more fire? How does it go? That it has taken all this time for the light to get to us. Something like that. So that what we are seeing, little sister, is like a memory of someone who has passed away.

No, tonight she is mine. I reach and pick her up. I hold her to me closely.

The quiet one rests the rifle on his shoulder.

"Mmm," she says, indecisive. She is holding her forefinger to her lips. And then she sees it. "There," she says. She points between the peaks of pines.

"You sure?" I ask her. I want it to be perfect. I want her to be happy. It is a tiny star, not really red, not yellow, but pink, winking off and on.

"That's it," she whispers. She has her arm around my neck. She gently pulls my head to hers so I can look down her short finger to the sky. She whispers, "That's the one."

THE OLD AND THE LOST

For Logan Delano Browning

I was born in a land of bayous, raised between rivers. There is a place in Southeast Texas where two rivers meet and become one. There is a long bridge over these waters, and as you drive across, you can look to the south and see where the Old River and the Lost River become the Old and the Lost. You can look out as far as you can see and watch this wide water become the bay.

There is a small town just north of this bridge where my father and his father were born. My father and his brothers were raised between these rivers. His brothers, my uncles, were older, and both of them left without teaching him to swim.

When the Japanese attacked Pearl Harbor, my father and his brothers joined the armed services. One joined the Air Force, and one joined the Army, and because my father was the youngest, and because he was determined to be his own man, he joined the Navy. There was a small problem. My father was afraid of the water. The Navy tried and tried to teach him to swim—ordered him to dive off the decks of ships, ordered him to jump out of tall towers—but he couldn't learn, so they stuck him in the *Segundo*—they stuck him in a submarine—and when he reminded them that he couldn't swim, they told him not to worry. They told him not to worry about it. They told him that if anything happened way down there, he wouldn't *need* to swim. They told him that if anything happened down there at the bottom of the ocean, he'd be dead anyway.

When I heard about the hurricane, I called the airport to book a flight, and they asked me if I was crazy. They asked me if I was insane, so I jumped in my truck and headed south. Through Virginia and Tennessee. Through Mississippi and Louisiana. Twenty-four hours. Back to Texas. Down the old highway. Orange. Beaumont. China. Nome. Past pasture after pasture. Past abandoned airstrips. Closed cattle auctions. Devers. Raywood. Ames. Past rice field after rice field where the farmers went broke. Past soybean field after soybean field where the farmers went broke. Past Brahma bulls. Billboards stripped bare by the storm. Deserted dryers. The elevators where they stored their grain. The tall, white towers like castles of the late King Rice until the king died, and the workers moved away, and the fields lay fallow up and down the highway.

I drive across the Old and the Lost and back to Sour Lake. I drive down Main Street, around the courthouse, around the square, and think of the Hoffmans. And then I drive to the end of the road.

This is what I remember. I remember a big house with columns, a long lawn lined with live oaks, a driveway that ran up under the porch. I remember the low limbs of the live oaks, the hanging Spanish moss that hid the house from the road. And I remember the family.

The father and the mother owned stores on the square. The father sold expensive suits to Southern gentlemen. The mother sold pretty dresses to Southern ladies. His store was on one side of the courthouse. Her store was on the other side. My father and my mother did not shop at these stores.

What I remember about the parents is that they were always

dressed up. The father always wore a coat and tie—even in the summer—a different suit every day. The mother always wore pretty dresses. My mother said that was easy when you owned the store. My mother said that if she owned the store, she'd wear pretty dresses too. Even the old Negro wore a bow tie.

What I remember about the family is that they were always smiling. The father. The mother. The little girl with the thick black hair. The little boy with the thick glasses. My mother said that was because they had money. They had the nicest house, they wore the nicest clothes, and they were smiling. People were always asking me what I wanted to be when I grew up, and when they'd ask me, I'd tell them, "When I grow up, I want to be happy." Of course, everybody hated the Hoffmans. But to me, as a small boy, in a small town, they were the royalty. They were the king and queen of Sour Lake. Every Saturday, I would follow them from a distance as they walked downtown to the depot, and every Saturday, I would wait on the platform for the train which would take them to their special church in Houston.

I remember climbing the low limbs of the live oaks and watching the children play. A little girl and a little boy. Grayson and Gregory. She wore braces on her teeth. He wore braces on his legs.

Every Sunday afternoon, they played on the long lawn. The old Negro carried the set from the garage. He stuck stakes in the ground. He stuck a stake at one end of the yard, and then he stuck a stake at the other end. The stakes were painted with pretty stripes. Blue. Red. Black. Yellow. Green. Orange. He stuck these white hoops into the ground. He made measurements. He positioned them carefully. Some on this side of the yard. Some on the other side. He brought out the picnic table and the chairs and placed them under the live oaks. He brought out a great big pitcher of tea.

And then the front door flew open, and then the little girl ran out, with her long black hair, with her bright red bows. The mother right behind her, laughing onto the lawn. And there was the little boy, holding onto the door frame, walking out on his stiff legs. The father standing behind him to catch him if he fell. The two of them wearing the same striped coats, the same striped trousers, which looked more like pajamas than Sunday school clothes.

The old Negro walked out onto the lawn. He handed the children their long wooden hammers. He handed them their painted wooden balls. The little girl was always red. The little boy was always blue. The father and the mother sat down in their chairs. The old Negro poured the tea, and then the children started. They hit their balls. They started at the stake at one end of the yard and ended at the stake at the other end. They hit their balls through the hoops. They took turns. The little girl, shrieking, running across the lawn, swinging her hammer between her legs. The little boy, hobbling to the next hoop—the head under his arm—using his hammer like a crutch. The old Negro, "Some more tea, Ma'am?" The mother, "Please." The father, "Thank you." *Smack*, the little girl slapping her ball across the lawn. *Tap*, the little boy shuffling along behind her. The little girl screaming when she cleared a hoop. The little boy knowing he would never catch her. The mother, "Grayson, slow down a little, Sweetheart." The father, "Gregory, you're doing just fine, Son." Until finally, invariably, the red wooden ball rolled up against the blue wooden ball. The little girl cheered. The little boy frowned. The mother, "Sweetheart?" The father, "Don't." The old Negro, "Miss Grayson, you be nice, now." But before he could replace his pitcher, before the parents could rise from their chairs, the little girl placed her bright red shoe on her red wooden ball and sent the blue wooden ball sailing into the trees. The mother, *"Grayson."* The father, *"Let him get it."* The little boy, without pouting, without complaining, limped off into the live oaks. The little boy disappeared into the Spanish moss.

The sun was going down. It was getting dark. The little girl cleared another hoop and cheered. The father and the mother watched the trees. The mother took his arm. The father took her hand. There was no breeze. There was no movement in the moss. The pocket watch ticking in his jacket. The ice cubes settling in their glasses. The mourning doves cooing in the dusk.

The old Negro dropped the pitcher of tea. "Mister Gregory!" he shouted. He started running across the lawn. He stopped at the low limbs of the live oaks. He parted the thick drapes of the Spanish moss and said, "Mister Gregory?"

I stand on this lawn fifty years later. There are no croquet wickets now. No wooden mallets. No painted balls. There are only wheelchairs and walkers scattered across the yard. There are school buses up and down the driveway. An ambulance parked underneath the portico.

Early Classical Revival. Four Doric columns. The twin side wings were added after the Revolution. The Texas Revolution. What were they thinking? Too big of a house for the Hoffmans. The builders, the first family, were not farmers. They did not sow the rice. They did not harvest the rice. They did not own the fields. They owned the canals, and they owned the water in the canals. They dug these ditches to the Old and the Lost and provided irrigation to those who could pay. My grandfather rode these levees on horseback. He monitored the gates for the men who sold these rivers. He made meticulous measurements. One quarter of an inch. One eighth of an inch. One sixteenth of an inch of water.

I have memorized this mansion. The storm shutters stripped away. The windows shattered. The pediment plastered with leaves. I walk across the lawn. I see the water line on the columns. The dirty rings of debris. The tidal surge must have been ten feet high. The azaleas killed by the salt water. The ambulance submerged.

The same front door. The same lion-faced knocker. I step inside. Two firemen splash past me and disappear into the darkness. The foyer is under water. One inch, maybe two. I hear the groaning of the generators. I hear the humming of the box fans. I hear someone shouting, "We need somebody to run into town!" The foyer smells like salt water, dead fish, and urine. A black orderly with a push broom sweeps the water outside. I hear someone shouting, "We need somebody to get us some gas!" There is a reception desk, and there is another push broom propped up against it. There is a wall of filing cabinets. Their drawers open. Their files missing.

A police officer walks up behind me. "You work here?" he says.

"No," I say.

"Then get the fuck out of the way," he says.

I turn to face him, eye to eye.

"*Please*," he says and shoulders past. "Who needs the hearse!"

A large black woman shouts from the landing, "Get rid of that water!"

"Yes Ma'am," the orderly says.

"Can you help me!" I shout over the sound of the sweeping.

"I doubt it!" she shouts back.

"I'm looking for someone," I say.

"Good luck!" she says. She's holding a clipboard. She's wearing a white dress. White stockings. She starts storming down the stairs. "Where's Daunte!" she shouts.

"Taking his break," the orderly says. He looks like he's getting ready to run.

She walks up to him through the water. She swats him with the clipboard. "Go get his ass," she says, "and tell him there ain't no more breaks!" She drops the clipboard on the desk. "Give me that!" she says and snatches his broom. She starts sweeping. "You gone stand there," she says without looking at me, "you gone get wet!"

I step out of her way. "I was hoping you could help me," I say.

"Honey," she says, "we're *long* on hope around here." She pushes the water through the front door. "But we're mighty *short* on help."

"What happened?" I say. "The lake get up?"

"Do what?" she says. She slaps the push broom on the steps.

"All this water," I say. "Did the lake get up?"

She stops sweeping. She just looks at me. "What's wrong with you?" she says.

"Pardon me?" I say.

She walks back to the base of the stairs. "Did the lake get up!" she says. She starts sweeping. "The lake *don't* get up," she says. "The lake *can't* get up. It's a lake!"

"But all this?" I say. "All this water?"

"Every now and then," she says, "them rivers bleed together and drown this whole country."

"The storm," I say. "Didn't the hurricane come up in here?"

She stops sweeping. "Where you from?" she says.

"Here," I say.

"Here?" she says.

"Sour Lake," I say.

"I doubt it," she says. "We don't tolerate no stupid children. You musta been adopted." She grabs the other push broom. "Till he gets back, you get to be Daunte," she says. "You two could be related."

I show her my cup. "Do you have someplace I can put this?" I say.

She nods to the desk. "What is it?" she says.

"A milk shake," I say.

"Where'd you get that?" she says. "Who's got electricity?"

"Beaumont," I say.

"Beaumont," she says. "Beaumont's got electricity."

"Can I put this someplace?" I say. "Someplace cold."

"What're you asking me?" she says. "Do I got a icebox?"

"Do you have an icebox?" I say.

"I gotta bunch of iceboxes!" she says.

"But not for me," I say. "Not for *my* milk shake."

"Not for *nobody's* milk shake!" she says. "We don't got electricity! We don't got water! We don't got gas! You understand?"

"I understand," I say.

"Even if we *had* electricity," she says, "we can't go storing some-body's milk shake! We got supplies. We got treatments. We got medications for our residents." She reaches for the cup. "I say we split it," she says, "before it melts."

I set the milk shake on the desk. "It's not for me," I say. "It's not mine to share."

She hands me the broom.

"Where's your help?" I say.

"You're it," she says, and we push the rivers back outside. We sweep the white tile clean, and before we can move our brooms, the dark water covers it again.

I look around the foyer. "Where is this coming from?" I say.

"The rivers, the bay, the Gulf of Mexico," she says. "Pick."

"Did you leave?" I say.

"We wanted to leave," she says. "We needed to leave. We called and we called, but nobody came. The police department didn't come for us. The fire department didn't come. And then we lost our electricity. And then we lost our phones."

We slap our brooms under the portico. "Everybody was at Happy Valley," she says. "Everybody was at the golf course. The police and the fire department. Rich people don't like to get wet!"

"Did they evacuate you?" I say.

"Not till they got everyone else," she says. "The country club got police cars and fire trucks and ambulances. We got school buses."

We slosh through the foyer. "We're not doing any good," I say.

"You're lucky you ain't working for me," she says.

"Why's that?" I say.

"I'd fire your whiny ass!" she says.

"What about your patients?" I say. "What about your residents?"

"We took them where we could," she says. "All the way up 105 to Cut and Shoot. We dropped them off where there was room. Saratoga. Batson. Moss Hill. Cleveland. When we got to 45, the interstate was a parking lot. Bumper to bumper. Galveston to Dallas. Three hundred miles. One terrified traffic jam. Nobody moving. Nowhere to go. One hundred degrees. One hundred ten. We just sat there and cooked. No air conditioning. Everyone ran out of water. Everyone ran out of gas. People lost their dogs on that hot highway. People lost their children. We lost six of our residents in them school buses. And then the sun went down, and the storm came in, and we closed up our windows and just sat there in the dark while that hurricane kicked the hell out of us."

We start sweeping.

"It sounds like you did what you could," I say.

"We saved who we could," she says. "We got the rest upcountry."

"Did you go back for them?" I say.

"We ran out of gas," she says. "Everybody ran out of gas. *The gas stations ran out of gas.*"

"But after the hurricane?" I say. "After the storm?"

"We didn't know where to look," she says.

I stop sweeping. "You didn't keep record!" I say. "You didn't keep track!"

She slaps her broom on the steps. "We were running from this water!" she says. "We were racing that storm! Did we keep track! We kept them old folks out of harm's way! We found safe harbors for all but the six! We held their hands through the hurricane!" She props her broom against the house. "We fanned them all day," she says. "We sang hymns all night. We prayed all the way through the storm. We just sat in them school buses and watched them die."

We hear them laughing before we see them. They are walking up the driveway. When they see us, they toss their cigarettes into the azaleas.

She shakes her head. "Daunte," she says.

"Yes Ma'am," Daunte says.

"You are one worthless nigger," she says.

"I know, Mama," Daunte says.

She hands her push broom to the orderly. I hand mine to Daunte. "Get to sweeping," she says. "Push them rivers back to the bay."

She grabs her clipboard, I grab my milk shake, and we step out under the portico.

"Why don't you let me drink that," she says, "before you go and melt it!"

The sun is going down, and what is left is streaming through the hanging Spanish moss.

"I'm looking for someone," I say.

She shows me the clipboard. "Does this someone have a name?" she says.

"Fannin," I say. "James Walker Fannin. He's my father."

"Fannin," she says. "Mr. Fannin. I remember Mr. Fannin."

"Do you have him?" I say. "Is he here?"

"Oh, Honey," she says, "I couldn't tell you."

"You can't tell me?" I say. "You don't know?"

"I don't know *who* we got," she says. "What I *know* is this. Who we got is safe and sound. Who we got is high and dry."

I point at the clipboard. "Is he on there?" I say.

"Maybe," she says. "Maybe not." She lifts the clipboard. "But this," she says, "don't mean nothing! This don't mean a thing!"

"Mama," Daunte says, "this old water must be up in these walls!"

"Shut up and sweep!" she says.

"Was he here?" I say. *"Was he on the buses?"*

"If he was here," she says, "he was on the buses."

I point at the clipboard. "May I see that?" I say.

"Help yourself," she says. "We got them babies all over the place. At other hospitals. At other homes. We got old folks now we didn't have then. They got dropped off. They got deposited. No identification! No papers! We don't even know their names!" She looks out over the lawn. *"Daunte!"* she shouts. *"Goddamnit to hell!"* She starts jogging across the yard.

"Yes Ma'am?" Daunte says. He steps outside.

"Help me!" she shouts. I look out across the lawn. The walkers.

The wheelchairs, and in one of them, a frail body slumped over the side.

"Pratt!" Daunte says. He starts running, still holding his broom. The orderly steps outside, and the two of us start running. We catch up with her, and we all reach the wheelchair together. "Miss Bernadette," she says, "where you been?"

Miss Bernadette is just sitting there, staring straight ahead. She looks like she has been waiting underwater.

"Pratt," she says, "take her inside."

"Yes Ma'am," Pratt says. He scoops up Miss Bernadette and cradles her in his arms.

"Daunte," she says, "take her chair."

"Yes Mama," Daunte says, and we all walk across the yard.

I scour the clipboard for my father.

When we reach the portico, she says, "I'm gonna need that back."

I point to a name that has been crossed off with magic marker.

"I didn't do that," she says.

"What does it mean?" I say.

"Nothing good," she says.

Pratt starts up the stairs with Miss Bernadette. Daunte starts sweeping.

"Listen, Honey," she says, "I hope you find him, but I got my hands full." She steps behind the desk. She opens a drawer. "Whoever we got," she says, "we got upstairs. We had to move them up out of the water just in case the city turns the juice on." She hands me a flashlight. "You're welcome to look," she says. She walks down the hallway and disappears into the darkness. "But you're on your own."

"Don't I know it," I say.

I climb the steps to the landing. They have installed a gate to keep the residents from falling down the stairs. I shine the flashlight to the right and to the left, to the east and to the west, down the dark hall.

Pratt emerges with Miss Bernadette. "No beds," he says.

I open the gate for him, and then I step through.

"Daunte," he says, "where you want her?"

I start down the hallway. An elderly woman appears before me. She is wearing a muddy nightgown. She is wearing her white hair past her shoulders. She grabs my arms with her long nails. "Charlie?" she says.

"No Ma'am," I say.

She releases me and shuffles away.

The walls of the hallway are lined with wheelchairs. Most of the residents have straps across their chests to keep them from falling over. Some blink when I shine the flashlight in their eyes. Some do not blink.

I stop at each door and step inside.

"Margaret?" a man says.

I shine my light on him. He is sitting on the bed with his legs over the side. He is barefooted. He is wearing pajamas. "Margaret," he says, "is that you?"

"No Sir," I say and walk away.

Someone touches my arm in the darkness. "Is it over?" she says. "Is it coming back?"

"It's over," I say. There is a train of wheelchairs behind me. "Are we leaving?" someone says.

"Not yet," I say.

The names on the doors have been crossed off, and other names have been written on the doors. Someone has drawn question marks with magic markers.

There is a room decorated with antique cars.

There is a room decorated with angels.

There are box fans in the windows. Extension cords to the generators.

I hear her downstairs. "Daunte!" she shouts.

"Yes Ma'am!" Daunte shouts.

"We need somebody to run into town!" she shouts. "We need somebody to get us some gas!"

An old gentleman greets me in a coat and tie. He is weaving over his walker. "Are you looking for Mr. Milam?" he says.

"No, thank you," I say, and he hobbles away.

I step into a quiet room. "Daddy?" I whisper.

"Not here," a frail voice replies.

I walk to the end of the hall. The room is dark. The drapes drawn. There are picture frames resting on the floor. Photographs leaning up against the wall. I shine the flashlight on each one of them. My father's father. His brothers. His *Segundo*.

I step inside. "Daddy?" I say.

He's lying on his side, facing the fan, his back to me.

I clear my throat.

There is a chair by the door for the breeze. The milk shake has melted, so I sit and find the straw.

I hear something out back. The generators start to stutter.

"Hey!" someone shouts down the hallway.

The box fan begins to die.

"Generators down!" someone shouts.

"Goddamnit!" she shouts. "Goddamnit to hell!"

I hear everything now. The creaking of the wheelchairs. The rubber stoppers of the walkers. "I'm ready," someone says. The wheezing. The heavy breathing. "Mr. Milam?" someone whispers.

"No," I whisper. "Sorry."

A collective sigh through this silence.

He turns in his bed. He rolls onto his back and groans.

I can't see him in the darkness. I can only see his silhouette. "Sure is a lot of groaning over there," I say.

"I got a whole hell of a lot to groan about," he says and starts coughing.

"Want me to get you some water?" I say.

"I don't want to see no water again!" he says.

"I don't doubt it," I say.

"How long you been here?" he says.

"Thirty minutes," I say. "Maybe an hour. Your milk shake melted, so I drank it."

"Help yourself," he says.

"I done did," I say. "It's gone."

He starts again. He sounds like he's coughing up his lungs. He's trying to get up on his pillow. He's trying to prop himself up.

I stand and start across the room.

He points. "Sit!" he says. His voice hoarse.

"You all right?" I say. "You don't *sound* like yourself."

He tries to clear his throat. "I don't *feel* like myself," he says.

"Want me to call you a nurse?" I say. "Want me to call you a doctor?"

"There ain't no nurses round here," he says. "There ain't no doctors. They all got sent to Galveston." He pulls back the drapes and spits out the window. "I don't guess we're worth saving."

I hear something behind me. I turn and find an old man standing in the doorway. He's leaning forward. He's holding a cane in each hand. He looks like he's been swimming in his nightshirt. "Mr. Milam?" he whispers.

"No!" I say and shoo him away. I look back to the bed. I squint through the darkness. "You sick?" I say.

"I just got the crud," he says.

"What all's wrong with you?" I say.

"I don't know," he says. "*They* don't know. They thought it was a stroke. They thought it was Parkinson's. And now they think it's MSA."

"Multiple sclerosis?" I say.

"Atrophy," he says. "Multiple Systems."

"Atrophy?" I say.

"Multiple Systems Atrophy," he says.

"Do I want to know what that means?" I say.

"Piece by piece," he says, "part by part, God's shutting my ass down."

91

"He does that," I say.

"He's been after me my whole damned life!" he says.

"He found you," I say.

"Multiple Systems Atrophy," he says. "It's just a fancy way of saying I'm dying."

"When'd you get back here?" I say.

"I couldn't tell you where 'back here' is," he says.

"Sour Lake," I say.

"Sour Lake," he says. "Why the hell not! Another backwater!"

"Beats being swept out to sea!" I say.

"I wonder," he says. "I wonder. They should've wheeled me out to the end of a pier. They should've chained my chair to a live oak tree. They should've let that storm come in here and take me." He pulls back the drapes and looks outside. "Sour Lake," he says. "Dead can't be no worse than this!"

"Where'd you think you were?" I say.

"Ever since the storm," he says, "I been in church houses, hospitals, high school gyms. I been in rest homes, nursing homes, old folks homes. I been in police cars, fire trucks, school buses. I shit you not— I couldn't tell you what state I'm in!"

"But they came for you," I say. "They got you out."

"Not for a while," he says. "Not for a while. They let us wriggle. They let us writhe."

"I heard about the buses," I say. "I heard about the highway."

"We just sat in our rooms and watched our televisions," he says. "We watched the hurricane leave the Atlantic, come into the Caribbean, move into the Gulf. The Leewards. The Windwards. The Greater Antilles. We heard that it was a big storm, a mean monster, a category three. The reporters said that there would be a surge. The reporters said that we should get the hell out. The reporters said that if we didn't get out, we wouldn't get out. The ferries would be shut down. The drawbridges closed. The evacuation routes flooded. We just sat in our rooms and watched our televisions."

"Two hundred," he says. "One hundred. Fifty miles out. And then the storm stopped. It just stopped. It just sat out there and strengthened. Category four. Category five. It crept up and down the coast. And we just sat there. We just sat there and waited. This was the day before landfall. This was the night before they came for us. And then the storm started coming in, and the lights started going out, and everyone started screaming."

"But they evacuated you," I say.

"Not for a while," he says. "They herded us into the hallway. They rolled us in our wheelchairs. They rolled us in our beds. They crammed us in like cattle in a car. The wind was blowing. The windows were breaking. They closed the doors up and down the hallway, and we just sat there in the dark and waited. Everyone was screaming and shouting. Everyone was crying and praying. And when those buses came, they piggybacked us out through the night. They carried us in their arms like little babies."

"I came as soon as I heard," I say. "I drove twenty-four hours."

"You came a long way for nothing," he says. "You wasted your trip."

"Probably," I say.

"Where you been?" he says.

"Away," I say. "I been away."

"No shit?" he says.

"It's been a long time," I say.

"Who are you?" he says.

"I had to get out of here," I say. "I had to leave this place."

"Must be nice," he says. "Did it help?"

"Not so much," I say.

"It never does," he says.

"I was in such a hurry to leave everything behind," I say.

"You never can," he says.

"I brought everything with me," I say.

"You always do," he says, and he starts coughing. He starts coughing, and he can't stop.

I stand and walk into his bathroom. I find a cup on the sink. I turn on the faucet, but nothing comes out.

"Sit down!" he shouts. "Sit your ass down! We ain't got no water! We can't even flush the commodes!"

The sun has gone down. It is dark outside. It is dark inside too. I shine the flashlight along the wall. "I see you got your *Segundo*," I say. "I see you got your submarine."

"What's that?" he says.

"Your pictures," I say. "They must have taken them down before the storm."

"Those ain't mine," he says.

"Pardon me?" I say. I shine the light on the bed.

"Those were his," he says. "That other poor bastard."

"What!" I say. I walk across the room.

"Sit down, Goddamnit!" he shouts.

"Shut up," I say. I shine the light on him. He turns his back to me.

"Come here," I say. I grab him by the shoulder.

"Go away!" he screams. "Go away!"

I roll him over. I shine the light on his face. "Who are you?" I say.

"Who am I!" he says. *"Who the hell are you!"*

I let him go. I walk across the room and fall into the chair. "Somebody's son," I say.

"The Navy guy," he says. "The sailor."

"Submariner," I say.

"He's gone, boy," he says. "He was gone before I got here."

"What happened to him?" I say.

"What will happen to me," he says.

I grab the armrests and push myself up.

"You don't have to leave," he says.

"You were right," I say. "I came a long way for nothing."

I move the chair and step into the hallway.

"Don't go!" he says. "I was enjoying the company! We were getting along!"

I walk into him in the darkness. He shines his light on me. "Milam?" he says. "Benjamin Milam?"

I shine my light through the door. "He's in there," I say. "He's been waiting for you."

Someone has left the gate open. I make my way down the stairs. The foyer is dark. The floor is dry. The push brooms are propped up against the front door. "Hello?" I say. I leave the flashlight on the reception desk. "Hello?" I step out under the portico.

There is a full moon shining on the lawn. I hear voices out back, crickets in the azaleas, cicadas in the live oaks. I hear the generators kick in like the rigs on the interstate. I hear the cheering back behind the house.

I walk across the lawn. I right the walkers and the wheelchairs. Too many of these majestic trees were destroyed by the storm. The long, low limbs of the live oaks snapped. The bright white meat of the trunks exposed. I disappear into the Spanish moss.

Fifty years ago, moving vans disturbed this sleeping town. The trucks arrived first thing in the morning. The movers packed what they could. They loaded all day. The Hoffmans abandoned their stores on the square. The father said goodbye to his fellow businessmen. The little girl said goodbye to her friends at school. The mother sat at the picnic table and stared across the lawn. The movers were hurried, the movers were rushed, and when they left late that night, the tops of their trucks tore the limbs from these trees.

The Baptist church held a service that night. The whole town came. The Hoffmans had left. My mother dressed me in my Sunday school clothes. And when it was over, I didn't walk home. I walked to the big house at the end of the road. There was a bright moon high up in the sky. Someone had hung black sheets on the columns. Someone had hung a black wreath on the door.

I walked up the dark drive. I stepped over broken limbs and branches. I started off across the yard and tripped over something.

I could see the croquet set still standing on the lawn. I could see the white wickets shining in the moonlight.

I walked to the picnic table and selected a mallet. I selected the blue ball, and I began to play. I knew to start at one end of the yard. I knew to hit the ball through the wickets. But this was all I knew. I didn't know if I should head off to the left. I didn't know if I should head off to the right. I decided that it didn't matter. I decided that this was my chance, this was my time to play.

I didn't hear the front door open, I didn't see him step outside, but I did hear someone sobbing, someone weeping under the portico. And then I saw him, and then he saw me, and he started running. I started running too. I didn't even drop the mallet. I just ran. I hurdled the wickets and headed for the trees.

"Hey!" he was shouting. "Hey!" He was chasing after me.

I ran into the live oaks. I hid myself in the moss.

I could see him. He wasn't running. He wasn't shouting. He was walking now across the lawn. I could see him in the moonlight. I could hear him singing, "Come out, come out, wherever you are!" I could see him parting the thick drapes of the Spanish moss. I could hear him whispering, *"Mister Gregory, where are you, Honey?"*

FICTION TITLES IN THE SERIES

Guy Davenport, *Da Vinci's Bicycle*
Stephen Dixon, *14 Stories*
Jack Matthews, *Dubious Persuasions*
Guy Davenport, *Tatlin!*
Joe Ashby Porter, *The Kentucky Stories*
Stephen Dixon, *Time to Go*
Jean McGarry, *Airs of Providence*
Jack Matthews, *Crazy Women*
Jack Matthews, *Ghostly Populations*
Jack Matthews, *Booking in the Heartland*
Jean McGarry, *The Very Rich Hours*
Steve Barthelme, *And He Tells the Little Horse the Whole Story*
Michael Martone, *Safety Patrol*
Jerry Klinkowitz, *Short Season and Other Stories*
James Boylan, *Remind Me to Murder You Later*
Frances Sherwood, *Everything You've Heard Is True*
Stephen Dixon, *All Gone: 18 Short Stories*
Jack Matthews, *Dirty Tricks*
Joe Ashby Porter, *Lithuania*
Robert Nichols, *In the Air*
Ellen Akins, *World Like a Knife*
Greg Johnson, *A Friendly Deceit*
Guy Davenport, *The Jules Verne Steam Balloon*
Guy Davenport, *Eclogues*
Jack Matthews, *Storyhood As We Know It and Other Tales*
Stephen Dixon, *Long Made Short*
Jean McGarry, *Home at Last*

Jerry Klinkowitz, *Basepaths*
Greg Johnson, *I Am Dangerous*
Josephine Jacobsen, *What Goes without Saying: Collected Stories*
Jean McGarry, *Gallagher's Travels*
Richard Burgin, *Fear of Blue Skies*
Avery Chenoweth, *Wingtips*
Judith Grossman, *How Aliens Think*
Glenn Blake, *Drowned Moon*
Robley Wilson, *The Book of Lost Fathers*
Richard Burgin, *The Spirit Returns*
Jean McGarry, *Dream Date*
Tristan Davies, *Cake*
Greg Johnson, *Last Encounter with the Enemy*
John T. Irwin and Jean McGarry, eds., *So the Story Goes: Twenty-five Years of the Johns Hopkins Short Fiction Series*
Richard Burgin, *The Conference on Beautiful Moments*
Max Apple, *The Jew of Home Depot and Other Stories*
Glenn Blake, *Return Fire*